Other Earth,
Other Stars

Books and stories by Marian Allen

Novels
Eel's Reverence
Force of Habit
SAGE Book 1: The Fall of Onagros
SAGE Book 2: Bargain With Fate
SAGE Book 3: Silver and Iron
Sideshow in the Center Ring
A Dead Guy at the Summerhouse

Short Story Collections
Lonnie, Me and the Hound of Hell
Turtle Feathers
The King of Cherokee Creek
MA's Monthly Hot Flashes: 2002-2009
Other Earth, Other Stars

Visit the author at
http://MarianAllen.com

Other Earth, Other Stars

Marian Allen

Per Bastet

Other Earth, Other Stars

Published by Per Bastet Publications LLC, P.O. Box 3023 Corydon, IN 47112

Cover Photo Courtesy of Rocky Raybell
Creative Commons license may be viewed here:
http://creativecommons.org/licenses/by/4.0/

Cover design by T. Lee Harris

ISBN 978-1-942166-14-6

Other Earth,
Other Stars

Contents

Space

1   Solo For Multiple Instruments

19   Out of the Frying Pan

23   Prime Date

25   Treasure of the Terra Madre

29   Best Ride in Space

31   Craw

Mermayds, the Species

35   Line of Descent

53   Out of the Cradle

57   Blood of Mermayds

71   Becalmed at Sea

Alien Earth

77   SMILE, Mr. President

81   Three Men in a Blimp, to Say Nothing of the Automaton

97   Dog Star

113   Sure Thing

117   Pile-Up

123   Western Star

125   Aardvark With an Arrow

131   Reading From the Book of First Bambi

133   Slob vs Snob

135 The One and Only
139 Til Death Us Do Part
153 Snow on the Screen
157 A Long Time Coming

Alien Worlds

163 The Woman Who Wasn't a Shave-Tail
183 Demon Ozone
185 Sanctuary
189 Mixed Metaphor
193 Independence
199 Leaving the Turtle

Space

Science fiction. Back in the "golden age" of the first pulp science fiction magazines, the term mainly conjured visions of spaceships and ray-guns. There are no ray-guns here, but the first group of stories in this collection take place in the artificial atmospheres of a ship, station, or habitat off the characters' native planet.

Apart from the first title, the stories in this section are flash (also called postcard) fiction, a form to which I'm partial.

Solo for Multiple Instruments

The solitude was appalling. She had agreed to it, had signed a waiver along with all the other paperwork for Volunteer Pioneers, had trained for a month with all her social circuits muted before leaving Earth, but the reality. . . . How could she have imagined the reality?

Tears overwhelmed Gale's eyes, flowing down her cheeks when she tried to blink them away. The other colonists in the dome's common room went about their business or pleasure, unaware of her distress. *At least,* she thought, *I could stand up and wail, and then they'd know. The people in other parts of the colony wouldn't know even then. I can't tell them. I can't reach them.* She blinked again and wiped her cheeks with her palms. She fumbled in her jumpsuit pocket for a tissue. *Gale Sanderson, cry-baby,* she thought scornfully.

"Hey." Toby Barnes, the Project Facilitator spoke aloud — well, he had to, didn't he? With no social circuits to connect their minds, out loud was the only way to talk. He sat down next to her on the couch, his voice soft and husky, warm and calm. "Just starting to hit you?" He tapped his forehead.

Gale nodded. "It—" The syllable came out thick and

rough. She cleared her throat and tried again. "It isn't as if I didn't know ahead of time. I knew. I was okay with it."

"Seemed like a good idea, didn't it, Sanderson?" Toby said. "Get some space for yourself." Toby — he was Dr. Barnes, officially, but said he preferred Toby — greeted every new colonist personally and apparently kept up a protective observation for a while after arrival.

She nodded and dabbed at her nose with her paper tissue, which was now in shreds.

Barnes handed her a handkerchief. "Kind of like asking for a little elbow room and finding yourself alone in the haunted castle."

She blew her nose and laughed uncertainly. "Hardly haunted."

"No?"

"My *brain*? Thanks, boss."

"That's how it hit me, anyway." He leaned forward, forearms resting on his thighs, gaze flicking around the common area. "That's how it still hits me. With the network, you're never alone with your thoughts, unless you want to be. Without the network, it's just you and memory and imagination. All these haunted castles, moving around each other, each one with one living resident looking out, trying to catch a glimpse of another living resident."

If she had still been connected, Gale would have passed that on to her network. Now, nobody would hear it but the two of them. It seemed a shame. It seemed a waste.

"They told me it was because I'd be too far from my network to pick up transmissions. But it seems like they could connect us all in a new network — just us in the colony. It would cost something to reconfigure everybody's software, but still. . . ."

"False economy," Toby said. "You're right. Keeping us in a network would be cheaper than mental health counseling to keep us from going buggy."

"Does the counseling help?"

The Facilitator looked at her over his shoulder and rolled his eyes around and around. "Why do you ask?"

She cackled. "Do it again," she said, and tapped the center of her left palm three times with a fingernail.

Toby looked away, so he didn't see her face when she remembered her *video on* signal wasn't going to work.

~*~

The planet had not been Terraformed. There had been talk of it, but sentimentalists and budget-watchers had united against it. Instead, there were what they called "containments": geodesic domes like blisters on the surface, connected by tunnels dug underground. They had brought anything they couldn't produce for themselves, and supply ships would bring more once a year.

"If we're still here in another year," Anouk Barronne said cheerfully.

After three days on site, Gale still automatically checked her useless social circuits for the emoticons that would tell her if Anouk were serious or joking.

She and Anouk, each tri-lingual in French, English and Esperanto, were on assignment in one of the culinary herb gardens.

The bunny slopes — as the staff called the domes where the neophyte Volunteers worked — had opaque shielding, the lighting entirely artificial. Newcomers to the colonies often felt threatened by a clear view of the alien landscape. Less often, they felt drawn to it, and some had been known to open a hatch and step out, in spite of unbreatheable air and unknowable pathogens.

"What do you mean, 'If we're here in another year'?" Gale checked the commissary order and broke off some dill fronds. The bright, thick scent almost made her giddy. Even after she sealed the harvest into a freshbag, the air and her hands were redolent with the herb's clear note.

"Because of the— What do you call them?" Anouk cocked her head, then grimaced.

With a not-entirely-compassionate pang of empathy, Gale realized Anouk had been trying to access a French/English dictionary site that wasn't available to her anymore.

Anouk frowned briefly, then said, "Gremlins. We have gremlins."

Does she even know what that means? Gale smiled at the secret freedom of thinking what she wanted as directly as she wanted. No checking to make sure she was thinking off-line, no worrying that she might have been hacked, her stream of consciousness broadcast on rogueband. It was this freedom, dimly dreamed, that had nudged her toward the Volunteer Pioneer program in the first place.

Anouk misinterpreted her smile. "It's true. Ever since construction started. Tools missing, equipment scratched and dented overnight, food contaminated. Once, a storage bin was found forced open and an atmo suit had been taken out of it and turned inside out. What do you say to that?"

"Sounds like somebody has a sophomoric sense of humor."

"Huh!" Anouk made one of her vast repertoire of unattractive sounds. "No one would contaminate food in space. Not for a joke."

"Sabotage, then."

The Frenchwoman gave an eloquent shrug—something

no emoticon could ever fully convey. "They say it was gremlins. They say we still have them. The ones who have been here the longest, they say it."

"They're just trying to intimidate us." Gale stopped working and stared at the skin of the dome, as if she could see through the shielding. "They're telling scary stories to the new kids."

"Perhaps," Anouk agreed, her voice implying that she didn't agree but didn't want to argue.

Gale shivered. It was, possibly, the most disconcerting thing about being off the network: having to pay such intimate attention to non-verbal communication with mere acquaintances and even strangers. No, worse was the feeling that other people were paying that kind of close attention to you.

~*~

Anouk had gone to use the "water box", as she insisted on calling it, and to bring them an afternoon snack. Gale worked her way toward the end of the row, trimming and packing dill for the commissary.

The closer she came to the dome surface, the stronger the feeling of being watched became. Her own reflection startled her, the apprehensive eyes so much wider than usual, the features blurred by the panel's semi-matte finish, colors leeched by the dull silver tint. *It's only me.* Gale met her own hazy gaze in the gray panel. *Or is it?*

She stared at her image on the thin barrier between the inside and the outside, at herself-that-was-not-herself, and her heart pounded, reveling in the presence of another consciousness.

"Hello," she said, suddenly fiercely curious about this new acquaintance. "Pleased to meet you. I would offer to trade profile locations with you, but that's a thing of the past, isn't it?"

"Ah, Dieu!" Anouk called from the doorway. "Don't start talking to yourself, my friend. That way lies madness." She handed Gale a thermal glass sipping mug of black coffee and a freshbag of three ginger snaps.

Embarrassed, Gale said, "I wasn't talking to myself. I was talking to the gremlins."

"I see." Anouk nodded and took a careful sip of the hot coffee. "Now, does that make you less mad, or more mad? And will you tell Toby Barnes, or do I have to. . . . What is the phrase? 'rat you out'?"

"Tell Toby? Why?" But she knew why. Anouk didn't even bother to answer. They couldn't afford to have anybody go off the rails in a pioneer site. One lunatic in a closed environment with such a limited population, so few of whom were expendable, could be a disaster. "Projecting oneself as a separate entity" was one of the things the counselor had specifically warned them about. Any instance — any suspected instance — was to be reported to one of the mental health staff or the Project Facilitator. She wasn't certain that one creepy moment meant her brains were scrambled, but nobody could afford to take that chance. She would have to tell Toby.

~*~

The counseling session was a little more crowded than she had expected. Doctors Paulo Battaglia (psychologist) and Folame Simisola (psychiatrist) were both present, which wasn't entirely surprising. Toby was there, too, which she hadn't anticipated, sitting behind her line of sight as if he were just a fly on the wall.

It made her nervous. The whole thing made her nervous.

Dr. Battaglia smiled reassuringly. "You aren't in trouble, you know, Ms. Sanderson," he said. "In fact, it speaks very well for your stability, that you reported this immediately. I hope that helps."

It did, actually. She relaxed.

"You say you felt you were meeting someone new?"

"I didn't look like myself. The reflection was. . . ," she held her hand up in front of her face and wiggled her fingers, "distorted. I guess that was the thing."

"It's very difficult," Dr. Simisola said, her voice smooth and kind, "and more difficult for some than for others, to lose the network. Some people feel . . . lonely, inside their own heads. Some of them. . . ." She trailed off and waved a pink-palmed hand at Dr. Battaglia. "Continue, please, doctor."

He nodded his appreciation, still smiling at Gale. "Did you fantasize any words? Actual words?"

Had she? It almost seemed she had, but. . . . "No, I don't think so. I think it was more of an impression. It *was* like the network. It was like somebody new popping up in your stream, you know? Like when you have the MagNet engaged, and you and somebody within each other's compatibility parameters come within six degrees of each other and *pop* — you're in chat together. It was like that. You know: There you are, and 'hello' is just a formality."

Dr. Battaglia's smile widened to show he understood. "How did you feel about that?"

"Surprised. Excited. Happy." She huffed a mirthless laugh. "Then stupid."

"No, no, no," Dr. Simisola protested gently, patting the arm of her chair in lieu of Gale's out-of-reach hand.

"No reason to feel negative about the experience," Dr.

Battaglia agreed. "It isn't uncommon. Many people — especially new arrivals — experience what we call a phantom network. With a phantom network, patients report a sense of a presence or presences inside the mind or body, thoughts not their own and not representing themselves as their own, sometimes actual words or phrases or whole conversations, usually with people they had known on the disconnected circuits."

"No, it was nothing like that. It was like meeting somebody *new*. Is that worse?"

Dr. Battaglia spread his hands. "No, indeed. You have nothing to worry about, young woman."

Dr. Simisola glanced over Gale's shoulder for the first time during the interview, to where Gale had heard Toby seat himself. "I tend to agree. Medication is not indicated."

Dr. Battaglia tapped the arm of his chair with a fingernail. "Counseling. . . ," he mused aloud. "Isolation."

"Isolation?" Gale sat forward in alarm. "What?"

"Just for a week or so. With counseling every day. Just until we're sure this is resolved."

"But. . . . Isolation?" Her breath nearly stopped, just thinking about it.

"Phantom network syndrome has proved highly contagious and highly disruptive, as you can imagine." Dr. Battaglia folded his hands across his stomach and leaned back, at ease and comforting. "You won't be entirely secluded, of course, Ms. Sanderson. Dr. Simisola and I will visit you every day; Dr. Barnes—" he nodded at Toby— "will visit you; nurses and orderlies will monitor you and tend to your needs. And, of course, you'll keep busy. I understand your Esperanto and French are quite good?"

At last, something she was sure of. "Yes, sir."

"We'll put you to work double-checking the translations of reports, then. Dry, but challenging. I think you'll find your mind pleasantly occupied, and these disturbing symptoms will just—" he fluttered a hand in the air, "—vanish."

~*~

For two days, Gale thought he was right. For two days, there wasn't a trace of anything in her head that recalled the wonderfully dear jumble of input she had thought she wanted to escape. She remembered her mother saying, "All those years of taking you three to lessons and practices and games and recitals and friends' houses and what-have-you, I looked forward to having my time to myself. Now you're all grown and gone, I miss it." Empty nest syndrome, she called it. *So what do I have — Empty head syndrome?*

From time to time, she felt herself under observation, but she had been told she would be, and she soon learned to ignore it.

For two days, she sat, with her back to the opaque dome, reading brief reports — essays, really — on basic scientific principles. The holographic monitor displayed three screens side-by-side, with the same report in English, Esperanto and French, and she was to read each one and mark any translation mistakes. There never were any.

It was obviously busywork, given to her to keep her mind occupied. It didn't matter whether she did it or not, but she did it.

On the third day, came the attack, for want of a better word.

She was jolted upright by a shock of pure joy and triumph. The sense of a lost friend found again was so strong, she bounced in her chair and thought, *U, u, u, u, u! Where u bin? Missed! Missed! And look! I see!* The ghost of another mind — only one, but more than just her own — tumbled around hers like a puppy — poured out happiness and excitement and thoughts she couldn't grasp, as if they were being sent in a language she didn't understand and had never heard before.

"Help," she whispered. Then, louder, she cried, "Help! Dr. Battaglia! Dr. Simisola! Toby! Help me!"

The "other mind" drew back, sending waves of calm. Her terror subsided as the doctors strode into the room, and she wept because she was ill, alone in her haunted castle.

~*~

"Don't worry, Sanderson." Toby had come down to her quarters to keep her company and distract her with an evening of chess. Neither one knew more than the basic moves, so they were evenly matched. "A lot of people have trouble adjusting. You get used to it. If you don't, what's the worst thing that can happen?"

"I go crazy."

Toby bounced a fragment of cookie off her forehead and spoke the sound effect: "*Doink!* No. Wrong. The docs wouldn't let you go crazy. They'll get you through this. Worst case: They hold you steady till the supply ship comes back, and ship you back to civilization. Some people just aren't cut out for this life, Sanderson. No shame."

She rested her head in her hand, her elbow on the table, and moved a pawn at random. "I don't understand why I can't just stay down here all the time. I never had any of those 'episodes' until I started working topside."

He frowned at the board. Without looking up, he asked, in a flat tone, "Was it really that bad?"

"No." Numb with desolation, she said, "It was great. Like a mirage in the desert. Looks like life, but there's nothing there." She watched Toby make a move, and said, not caring, "I think you won."

~*~

The next day, they gave her anti-anxiety drugs. Dr. Simisola dispensed the tablet in person, along with a sympathetic smile.

"Will this stop it happening?" Gale asked.

"Perhaps, or perhaps not. But it will mute the fright and distress if something *should* happen. We want you to open another holo-screen on your desk. If you have a recurrence of this conviction that you're being invaded, we want you to journal it." After a brief hesitation, she continued, "If you can. If you can't — if your thoughts are too chaotic to grasp, or if you begin to feel overwhelmed — call out, as you did yesterday. All right?"

~*~

Half-way through the day, she was given a set of essays she had seen before. The next set was a repetition, too — same text, same illustrations. As if the task hadn't been boring enough to begin with.

Nevertheless, the drug made her feel too dull to resent the brutal pointlessness of the assignment, and she plodded through the text again, in English, in Esperanto, in French. English, Esperanto, French.

It was working. The medication and the tedium made a perfect team. From the moment she sat down, she had that sense of being in company, but the feeling was muted. She was able to ignore it most of the time. There was an occasional spike of intense happiness but, by the end of the day, when she could retreat to her quarters, she had experienced nothing to log.

She dreamed of her work. The number of screens open in the air at eye-level changed. Sometimes there were three, sometimes four, sometimes five. When she tried to count them, to hold the number steady, she woke up. The dull dream of a dull mind worn out by a dull job.

~*~

"Today," Dr. Battaglia said in Gale's morning session with the doctors, "I would like for you to journal. Begin with your dreams of last night. And. . . ." He settled himself back in his chair, like a smiley-face emoticon taking any sting out of his words, "You meant it for the best, but you should have logged those bursts of emotion."

"I thought I was supposed to be ignoring them."

"We're seeing if we can't disconnect the phantom network. As long as you sense connections to other people, as if your social circuits were still active, we need to be aware of it." His warm smile drew one from her.

Dr. Simisola said, "It's true that the essays you're being sent are repeating. We'd like you to continue to read them through as usual, but if you get too bored to read consciously, feel free to journal spontaneously. Anything that comes into your mind. If you can separate and label the thoughts you recognize as your own and the ones you've assigned to this 'other', that would be particularly helpful."

~*~

She managed to get through most of the next day with no trouble. Although she had no place to post it and nobody to read it, Gale had continued to keep a journal after she entered the program. She called it onto the fourth screen and, in between sets of essays (Newton's Laws, Relativity Simplified, Refraction of Light), she dipped in and out of old entries.

Toby said it was like being alone in a haunted castle.
Gale read the journal entry and shivered.

She paged past everything that had happened since the initial onset of the syndrome. When she reached the current date, she inserted a holographic video she'd made of herself as a baby morphing into herself now, ending with the hologram she used as her virtual reality avatar. She reviewed the VR training program she had used before she decided to join the Volunteers, showing the planet from space, the landing pod sinking closer to the surface, seeing the domes from above, then from the ground. She watched her avatar board the shuttle, then saw, through her avatar's eyes, the off-kilter colors and shapes of the local landscape and foliage, which only looked like Terran colors and shapes because those were all she had as reference. Here, she inserted holograms of landscapes she knew, personally or through pictures.

The virtual shuttle entered the airlock dome and, after fast-forwarding through decontamination and atmosphere/pressure "normalization"—meaning, of course, Earth-normal—Gale's avatar shook hands with a smiling Toby Barnes and exchanged greetings and introductions.

She played that part three times.

"Hi!" Toby said, over and over. "Happy to have you here."

The program malfunctioned at that point, and she couldn't follow herself through the underground corridors, or access maps or blueprints of the facility.

She checked other maps and holograms of the planet, and they came up with no problem. She pulled up one of the exterior of Dome 16a, section 3, ward 7, cubicle 12, and found she could do a cut-away view. There was her avatar, sitting at the desk, working away. She rotated the perspective to watch her own face as she watched her avatar watch her avatar watching her avatar.

She watched herself smile, then she jumped as the program replayed her first handshake with the Program Facilitator.

Gremlins, she thought. *Here's one for Anouk's collection.*

Curious, she looked up "gremlins" in the mainframe dictionary. "Imaginary beings playfully blamed for causing mechanical malfunctions or bad luck."

The "other mind", which she had been not-quite-sure was lurking around, de-lurked.

Gale changed the font in her journal and typed, I am not gremlins. The castle is not haunted. Hi. Happy to have you here. Snoopy dancing.

"Help?" she said. "Help help help help help?"

She typed, **Who are you?**

There was a swirl of static in her mind, sounds and visualizations she couldn't understand or interpret.

The door opened and Toby and both doctors eased in. Gale, borne along on a wave of delight, said, "Hi. Happy to have you here. I'm not crazy, and you know it."

Her fingers itched and she typed what came into her head:

Sound record. Please. Relax.

She switched on the audio and closed her eyes.

The sounds she made weren't singing and weren't talking; she just made whatever sounds she felt compelled to make by the presence in her head. Some intelligible words from the scientific essay on her screens came out, but most of the vocal stream was just noise.

When she seemed to be finished, she opened her eyes and told her observers, "That wasn't me, by the way."

She clicked to the next set of essays, said, "That was *Elementary Principles of Optics*, by Dr. Prandash Gupta.

For my next selection, I'm going to do a little piece called *Thermodynamics*, by Dr. Bailey Dwyer, and it goes something like this."

At the end of the translation, her throat was scratchy and her voice was hoarse.

She was also at home with the entity visiting her. She smiled blandly at the doctors who waited breathlessly for what she would do next, letting them wait while she and her new friend held a private conversation.

I can't do any more today. I'll see you tomorrow.

`You aren't freaked? You know I'm friending you?`

I know. Thank you.

`Thank you back.`

She stood up and took three dizzy steps toward the door. Toby pushed between the other doctors and picked her up.

"You rat," she said.

~*~

"Phantom network syndrome is a very real condition," Dr. Battaglia insisted, pouring the four of them a second round of champagne.

"But I don't have it," Gale said, inhibitions loosened by the day and the bubbly.

"Ah," said Dr. Simisola, raising a manicured finger, "but we didn't know that. We could only hope."

Apparently, Gale's inhibitions weren't the only ones with their lids coming off. Dr. Battaglia gave his colleague a slight frown and a miniscule head-shake, then turned a bright smile on Gale.

They could only hope.

"That's why you disconnected our social circuits and

didn't wire us all together here. You didn't want anything to get in the way of. . . . Of what?"

"Interspecies communication," Toby said. "This planet looked empty of animal life, but. . . . Well, you've seen it. It's obviously just impinging on our visual acuity. Instruments built to increase our range of perception picked up shadows and echoes — enough to tell us there was certainly something here. But that didn't help us make contact."

"You needed a filter."

Dr. Battaglia sipped his champagne. "We needed a machine. This machine needed to be sensitive enough to pick up mental emanations, tough enough to stand the stress of sudden input, flexible enough to identify a wide range of possible inputs as significant, precise enough to tune in to the elements of significant input that it could work with and powerful enough to learn almost instantly. Fortunately, such a machine already exists."

"My *brain*? *My* brain?"

"Two brains," said Dr. Simisola. "One on our side, and one on theirs. The odds were against it ever happening, but—" She raised her glass in a salute to Gale.

Toby said, "Anybody who showed or reported signs of phantom network syndrome was isolated. If they were really suffering from a psychological aberration, we wanted to help them deal with that. If they were getting communications from the indigenous life-forms, we wanted to nurture that."

"Without letting them — say, without letting *me*, for instance — know what you were using them — using, for example, *me* — for."

Blithely, Dr. Battaglia said, "We couldn't risk

contaminating the experiment. If we had told you what we wanted—"

Dr. Simisola interrupted, "The human mind is staggering in its ability to create an elaborate construct and externalize it."

"But you made the breakthrough." Toby beamed fondly at her. "Against all the odds, you not only made the breakthrough but were able to embrace it and work it. You don't know how fantastic that is." He poured another round. "What a day! What a day!" He lifted his glass and motioned for the other three to do the same. "Interspecies communication!" he declared.

They all clinked glasses.

Gale clinked with them, making a mental list of all the rude words she could teach her new friend.

She smiled and sipped champagne, snug in the knowledge that none of her superiors had the least idea what she was thinking.

Out of the Frying Pan

The heat was extreme, dry and so intense it almost numbed us. Did you ever put your hand too close to the surface of a skillet, trying to test how hot it was? Was it ever so hot you didn't even feel it right away, your skin switching sensation off while your brain tried to figure out what had gone so inexplicably wrong?

It was that kind of heat: stunning. Mrs. Bissa and I ran palms over our bald heads, then showed our hands to each other, grimacing. Perspiration wicked away instantly, leaving behind a coating of salty grease.

Strangers at the beginning of the show, Bissa and I had outlasted and outcooked all the other women.

The actual air pressure, 92 times that of Earth, and the heat, nearly 1,000 degrees, were mostly offset by the ship's insulation and our distance from the surface of the planet, but the controls were set to continually ramp down. Every second, the pressure was a tiny bit stronger and the heat was a tiny bit worse.

Doesn't matter how hot it is: water won't boil with air pressure that high. It takes instinct and science to cook in those conditions, especially when the conditions constantly change.

A beep in my ear implant told me it was time for my private communication. I tapped the side of my head and Bissa nodded, busy with prepping her dish.

I closed myself into the comm capsule, which was just enough cooler than the rest of the satellite to make it a haven, make the other areas that much more hellish.

The monitor only goes one way. Why should the show pay for someone to interview us, when they can provide a list of pre-written questions for us to choose from and pretend we're being asked on the spot?

"I don't know what that Bissa bitch thinks she's doing. I mean, parsley? Really? We're way beyond garnish here."

I switched position. "Sure, I'm going to win! I'm Annika! Like I've said from the first: Annika wins!" I'm wearing as next to nothing as modesty allows, but I know the studio will splice in footage of my fans in their "Annika wins!" t-shirts. The show is behind that, of course. Marketing is king, after all.

"Bissa's a sad old woman. You know how cold-blooded seniors are; the heat probably feels good to her."

They were piping this to her as I said it. When her turn came, they would play what she said about me straight into my ear.

All too soon, the one-comm was over, and I left the capsule for the scorching kitchen area.

Mrs. Bissa wiped her hands and, with grim impassivity, moved to take her turn at the monitor. We slammed shoulders as we passed and had some harsh words and a shoving match. Did some name calling.

I could hardly keep a straight face. Today was the final episode: the pay-off. The cameras were always on us, but a muttered word here and there, a quick note on parchment paper, a gesture, a nod. . . . Today, we would throw away the contest, work as a team, and pull off a triumph of culinary science.

Why compete, when we could do so much better together?

Marian Allen

Prime Date

I'll never forget my first date with Brizno Enkler. Neither will you. That's right, we're *that* Mimzy Murgraff and Brizno Enkler.

When was it? *You* tell *me*. That's right, it was the first of Quarn, the Fifth Circuit of the Ascendant Serpent.

Yes, we really did meet for breakfast in the Doctoral University's Gifted Learning Center's cafeteria. Yes, it's true, I had scrambled protein and Brizno had waffles with blueberries from the hydroponic farm. He was back-to-nature even then.

Here's something you probably never heard: Brizno was a bit of a joker. He asked for two waffles and the dispenser gave him three. So, after we sat down, he offered the third one to me. I didn't want it. He picked it up and flung it across the cafeteria through the open door into the hall and shouted, "Look out! It's a UFO!"

We were all laughing when we heard this loud *snap* and the head poked through the door.

The room went nuts! Naturally, we knew what pterosaurs look like — pterodactyls, as the slang calls them — we'd spent long enough trying to raise viable clones, but we didn't expect to see one in the hall. The head looked enormous, sticking through the cafeteria door, sniffing for more waffles.

Dr. Giznikk stood up and shouted, "Who left the nursery bay door open? *Who?*" As if knowing would solve the problem.

"Oh, the poor thing!" I said. I grabbed a tray and ran to the dispenser. "Fifty waffles!" The dispenser flap pushed open, and at least a hundred steaming circles poured out, all over the tray and onto the floor.

Brizno brought another tray and, while I filled it with the overflow, he picked some up and skimmed them to the pter. *Snap! Snap!*

"What are you doing?" Dr. Giznikk waved his tentacles at us. "Too much carbohydrate! Do you want a flatulent pterosaur roaming the halls?"

"Sausage! Keep 'em coming!" Brizno called. I ordered a hundred sausage patties, and everybody grabbed some and tossed them out the door.

The pter withdrew its head, cleaning up the breakfast in the hall. Brizno shoved as much as he could onto one tray and plunged through the doorway. I was right behind him. While Brizno kept the pter's attention with the food, backing through the hall toward the nursery, I scrambled onto the 'saur's back and sang lullabies into its ear to calm it down. By the time we got back to the nursery, it was full of sausage and waffles and soothed with music, and the robonurses were able to get it back into its pod.

And that was how the Happysaurus Meal was born.

Treasure of the Terra Madre

All the children watched the monitors as the planet dropped away behind the ship. Not even the teachers thought it would be a more genuine experience if they had been able to see it, say, through a viewport in the rear of the vessel, supposing there had been one. This exact view, which was, of course, being recorded, was the one which would be replayed for as long as the name of "Earth" was remembered. The last view of Home with a capital H, a sight to bring tears to the eyes of generations yet unborn.

Ten years later, deep into the voyage to the next inhabitable planet, five-year-old Houston Naylor stared at his favorite thing in the universe: his father's paperweight.

"Can I hold it, Daddy? Can I look at it?"

Sometimes he could, and sometimes he couldn't. When Daddy was working, like now, he usually could.

Sure enough, Daddy was busy on his etab and didn't look up as he said, "Sure, buddy, sure. Be careful though, okay?"

"I'll be careful."

Houston hefted the small but heavy mounted sphere, marveling at how much weight such a small thing could have. He put it down and turned it on its axis, slowly, drinking in its beauty.

Most of it was deep blue. Daddy said that was water on the real thing. Daddy said the weird shapes and blobs and blips in other colors were land, and the different colors told you who the land used to belong to. It was also divided into grids by intersecting bands of gold; Houston thought those were probably like the walls of their family cubicles.

None of it belonged to anybody, now, Houston supposed, since there was nobody there anymore.

Just to be sure, he asked, "Who does the Earth belong to now, Daddy?"

"Doesn't belong to anybody now, buddy. The last people are here on this ship. We're going to find a new Earth. Be a long time before anybody could live on the old one again."

Houston, of course, knew all about faster-than-light travel. A baby could understand that, by the time the ship reached its destination, and they assembled the smaller ones that could carry just crews and pioneers, Houston would be old enough to be one of them. They learned in preschool that, by the time the pioneers got back to Old Earth, it would probably be lush and habitable.

He had asked Daddy so many times about the globe, he could rub his thumb over the blue and give the name of the gemstone it was made of: Lapis lazuli. He could touch the other colors and say: sandstone, agate, jasper, mother-of-pearl, jade.

"Is the Earth really made out of jewels, Daddy?"

Daddy was busy, but he surfaced enough to say, "Sure, buddy. Sure, sure."

"And nobody owns it now?"

"Nobody there. Look, could you go plug into the playtender or something? Daddy's really busy."

"Sure, sure," said Houston.

It was from that day that Houston knew what he wanted to do when he grew up.

Marian Allen

Best Ride In Space

"That rocker was my great-great grandmother's," Captain Thierry told the rare passenger or crewmember admitted to her private quarters. "The only thing I have of hers. Yes, I knew her; she was one of that last generation who did the longevity stuff."

Although the medical and technological ability to prolong productive and healthy lives still existed, few people took advantage of it anymore. Healthy lives, strong bodies, yes. But long, healthy lives, it turned out, made people either too conservative of their lives and health to take any risks or, on the other end of the spectrum, suicidally reckless.

"She was one of the first colonists to leave the solar system," the captain would say with pride. "One day, she's rocking little me in that chair, the next I know, she's a passenger on this very ship on her way to The Ark for 'The Ride To Take Humanity To The Stars.' She'll outlive me by at least a century. Crazy, huh? So she brought along a few things from home, but it turned out she overestimated the room she had in storage and she had to leave the chair behind. So I kept it."

A glider, not an actual rocker, it was bolted to the floor, and the cushions were Velcro'd in place. The captain liked to sleep in zero gravity.

Being captain meant the occasional night when concerns or a general sense of responsibility made it hard to sleep. Medication wasn't an option.

On those nights, Captain Thierry dialed down her thermostat and cocooned herself in a flannel blanket. She curled up in the chair, snaked one arm out to fasten down the web that would hold her in place, then pulled the arm and her head into the web. One good and well-practiced thrust against her restraint started the chair on an equal-and-opposite reaction glide. The lack of gravity countered the slight metal-on-oiled metal and molecule-against molecule friction, so the rocking continued for some time.

More than enough time for someone with a spaceship full of responsibility to rock herself to sleep in her great-great grandmother's wooden rocking chair.

Craw

Craw stomped along the station's corridor, unaware of his fellow colonists making way for him. He didn't hear them chuckle when he had passed, telling each other, "Craw's in one of his moods again."

He had done whatever he had to, to wangle a place in the ship, to fly to the stars, to live in flight in artificial gravity not-quite-Earth-normal. He had watched, studied, sold his soul for a chance to learn more, learn enough to be a medic.

It had been worth it. More than worth it.

Still, sometimes the safety suits made his shoulderblades itch. Sometimes the collar, with its emergency automatic atmoshield generator felt like he had a piece of plastic trash around his neck, strangling him.

Doc Aimanov always knew when Craw had had enough, and ordered him to take some time to recuperate.

"You're no good to the patients when you're like this. Go get it out of your system."

Craw reached his destination: the conservatory. The biosphere, the garden — whatever. It was the place the plants grew, that was all he cared about. A huge bubble of self-healing bio-fiber, it was a plant ecosystem all its own. He drew the warm, moist air into his lungs as if he hadn't been breathing before he entered the room.

He pulled off his gloves and clawed the rest of the suit off. It was a joke in the station: Ravi Crawford running naked through the jungle, though no one had ever seen a glimpse of his bare skin.

Three steps and he was hidden by the growth. Three more heartbeats and he was free, returned to his true form.

This was more like it! This was just what he needed! A couple of hours of this and he'd be ready to take on human shape again and mingle with the people, clever and unsuspected.

Meanwhile, he spread his raven's wings and flew.

Mermayds, the Species

Mermaids are creatures of fantasy. Mermayds, on the other hand, are sentient natural creatures. I created mermayds for my novel (out of print, as of the date of this collection's publication), EEL'S REVERENCE. The first two stories take place long before the novel. "Blood of Mermayds" takes place only a year or two before the novel, and "Becalmed at Sea" takes place not long after the novel's end.

Line of Descent

"No, this way," Goby told Grunion, his youngest nursemate. Grunion watched as the older mermayd flipped a cloud of silt up with his fluke, then doubled back and punched an imaginary shark with his fist.

Grunion mimicked him, stubby tail digging too deep and throwing up a chunk of rock. It didn't go very far.

"Better," Goby lied.

Grunion's tail was still only half his body's length, not quite long enough to balance comfortably on out of the water, and not long enough to use for much beyond simple swimming. Goby's tail was long enough to curl once and sit on, but it would be another year before it had enough length for him to move as quickly on land as an eel on the sea bottom.

"Watch me again! Watch me again, Goby," the tad said. Then he froze, drifting gently with the current, his eyes on something behind his nursemate.

Goby swiveled, prepared to fight, incredulous that a threat had gotten past the pod's sentries.

It wasn't a threat. It was Silversides.

Silversides took no notice of the two, of course; they were far beneath him. An anomaly among the mermayds, he set himself apart: never participating, never accepting or offering friendship, never sharing. He had been nurtured by a random passer-by, like everybody else, but he didn't even seem to have any feeling for his nurshen or nursemates.

He was followed by a line of his nurslings: five tads, one year apart — almost identical to one another, and almost identical to Silversides. His nurture pouch bulged with his youngest, which would undoubtedly be another copy. Again unlike other mermayds, all Silversides' nurslings were called Silversides, after their nurshen.

A mermayd's breeding habits were nobody's business, but. . . . Next year, the oldest Silverside tad would be a breeding adult, and that worried a lot of people.

Grunion swam closer to his older nursemate and murmured, "Goby, Goby, Goby."

Goby put an arm around the tad and patted him on the shoulder.

"I want to go home," Grunion said.

Goby left Grunion with their nurshen, a gray-haired, slow-moving elder named Manta. Manta hadn't taken a tad into his nurture pouch for years. Then, one day, he had been indifferently watching fish feeding on hatchlings when one of the newborns had run right to him and hidden in one of his braids, just behind his right ear. Manta had batted the baffled fish away and, bemused, stuck the hatchling into his nurture pouch. That had grown to be Goby. Afterwards, he had kept to his shelter during the Days of Emergence, but one year a hatchling had somehow found its way into his grotto. He always suspected Goby might have picked it up somewhere and, not old enough to nurture, had brought it to him. That one was Grunion.

~*~

Goby swam away from the pod. Everyone always warned against it, but almost everyone did it, anyway. The pod was settled for the season; hatching, with its rich feeding opportunity for predators, was long past; short-range rambling was relatively safe.

The only thing to watch out for now was the two-tails, and they were so rare they were nearly legendary. The old folks said they came in giant shells that floated on top of the lower sky. They had weapons, the elders said, that looked like sticks, and they sometimes hurt or killed a mermayd when they mistook one for a fish. That's what the old folks guessed, anyway. They said that mermayds had rescued a two-tails now and then, that had fallen out of its shell, and had tried to bring it to the pod, but it must always have been a sick one or an old one, because it had died before it had been brought very far.

Goby felt a disturbance in the currents. He moved upward, and found the turmoil stronger. The light grew no brighter as he approached the upper sky where the birds swam through the thin, impalpable substance called air. It was a storm, then.

He stuck his head above the surface, letting the wild waves take him for a swooping, directionless ride, while more water fell from above to join the sea.

Deafened by the racket of rain and wave, he didn't hear the two-tails' shell approaching, didn't see it until it was almost upon him. He wriggled away with a few powerful strokes of his tail and, turning head-down, plunged back into the serenity of deeper water.

His heart thudded. The shell had come so close! He could almost have touched it. He would have a fine boast to make to his peers, and it would be gratifying to compare his experience with those of the few others in the pod — all much older than he — who had also seen the shells pass.

With a crash he could hear, deep as he was, a two-tails plunged toward him. It wasn't swimming with purpose, though; it was thrashing with its arms and both its tails. Another sick one, fighting against its death. Its skin was loose and it had two scalps, one on top of its head and one under its mouth, both covered in thick black hair. Its loose skin sloughed off in pieces, and Goby realized it was artificial skin made out of something else, intended to protect the two-tails' real skin.

He had to admire its courage. How it struggled! It got its head turned upwards and its tails downwards. It flicked its tails separately and worked its way back toward the surface.

Maybe this one wasn't sick. Maybe this one fell out of the shell by accident — flung out by the storm waves. Maybe the shell would come back for it, if it could stay where the other two-tails could see it.

Drawn by curiosity and an urge he couldn't explain, an urge that had to do with helping life continue, he followed the two-tails up into the storm.

The creature flickered its tails and swept the water with its arms, trying to keep its head above the water. Waves washed over it, and it heaved its chest, making odd rasping sounds that seemed to push the water out.

Suddenly, Goby understood. The two-tails weren't like mermayds, who could tolerate air but needed the water. They were like whales and dolphins: They needed air or they would die. They didn't die underwater because they were sick or old, but because they couldn't breathe!

Impulsively, he grasped the animal around the waist and, undulating his tail, hoisted the two-tails farther out of the water. It jerked and cried out and stared at him with eyes unprotected from the spray by a nictating membrane, as his own were. It was a clever creature, though, and understood he wanted to help it. It put an arm around his shoulders and waved the other hand — a hand with no webbing between the fingers! — over its head, pushing a cry of distress out of its mouth that went, "Hi! Hi! Heer! Heer!"

The storm swept over them, and then was past. They watched it wash over the ocean until it was out of sight, carrying the shell with it. The shell didn't return.

And now what did he do with the thing? If he were right, and it needed air, he couldn't take it home with him. It would be unkind to leave it to sink, and he could hardly stay with it.

Not far away, there was a mountain that rose above the sky into the upper sky of air. Adult mermayds sometimes went onto the edge of it to dig clams or turtle eggs or to gather exotic fruit from the land plants. If two-tails were creatures of the upper sky, maybe land was familiar and safe to them.

Goby told the two-tails his idea and promised to take him to the land. The creature didn't understand, of course, but seemed to sense his good will, because it let him shift his hold, and it relaxed and allowed him to swim with it at the surface between the two skies.

It cried out when the land came into view. When Goby released it close to the shore, it lowered its tails and did something he would never have believed if he hadn't seen it for himself: It put its weight on its tails and, balancing on one and then the other, walked on its flukes as an octopus sometimes walks on its tentacles or a crab on its legs. In fact, those things Goby's people called two tails might be a form of legs. Or perhaps walking on its tails was a trick peculiar to this particular animal. It was an entertaining sight, anyway.

The two-tails made a sound at him, as if it were saying thanks. Goby raised an arm in salute and hurried for home.

~*~

Goby said nothing about the two-tails. It was tempting to brag about his encounter with one of the dangerous though delicate creatures, tempting to show off how he had solved the puzzle of their dying in spite of their would-be rescuers. And, if anyone doubted him, he could take them to the land and show them!

But then, of course, Manta and the other elders would be cross about his going so far from the pod alone and with no one knowing where he was. Manta would say *Why did I bother to nurture you? Why didn't I just pick up a piece of sandstone and put that into my nurture pouch?*

Even worse, the creature might be gone. Or he might have guessed wrong and the creature might be dead.

So he held his tongue and the days passed. He grew — all the tads grew, including the Silversides clutch. The youngest came out of the pouch, a fingerling that clung to his nurshen's hair and refused to associate with anyone who wasn't a Silversides.

"It isn't natural," Manta confided to Goby while Grunion played with other tads. "It isn't healthy. And that oldest nurseling will be parenting soon. He's your age, isn't he?"

Goby nodded. When Manta gave him a look of sudden realization, he couldn't hold back a bashful grin. Manta made an indulgent noise and gave him a rough hug.

"What'll it be?" Manta asked.

"Eggs," Goby said. He had been feeling a fullness just below where his skin blended into his scales. When he put a hand there, a slight swelling was barely noticeable.

Manta was long past producing egg or sperm, but the news made him look years younger. "Oh! I'll show you all the nicest places to deposit your clutch! It has to be somewhere fish can't get to them but sperm can. Somewhere there's a chance of someone taking one of your hatchlings to nurture before the predators snap them all up. My little tad — spawning! And in another year or two, you'll be wanting to nurture. I can hardly believe it."

It was embarrassing, being dragged around, shown off, discussed and made over by the adults in the pod. His only consolation was that his age-mates were suffering the same rite of passage. It made him feel very mature and very strong — a link in the chain of life that kept the pod vital. Little Grunion tagged along, his expression and his body language screaming of jealousy and admiration.

Only Silversides and his oldest avoided the community's excitement at the approaching reproductive season. Nobody ever saw them scouting the usual spawning sites, in spite of the fact that Silversides and his oldest were both more and more obviously heavy with eggs.

"What if you did?" one of Goby's age-mates — bearing seed, by the placement of his reproductive bulge — asked the others. They laughed nervously. "What if you did fertilize Silversides' eggs? I wonder who's done it before. Do you think he picks somebody and leads them to his clutch? I mean, it's *always* eggs with him, isn't it?"

"It happens," a spawner said. "My nurshen's nurshen—"

"It happens, but how often? Not very often. It's usually

one thing sometimes and the other thing other times. Almost everybody spawns some years and seeds some years. Sometimes both."

Another seeder said, "Nobody's ever *seen* him during the season. Nobody's ever seen him take a nursling; nobody's even seen him at a hatching, but he's always got one in the pouch when the hatching's done."

This was unnerving, like so much about the Silversides.

Disturbing though it was, it became a game among the seeders to follow the Silversides whenever they came across them, as if competing to see who would fertilize the superior Silversides clutch. Even some of the spawners played, hanging back so their condition wouldn't alert Silversides and his brood to the joke. As the season grew nearer, the two older Silversides would leave the younger ones in care of an elder and swim together, seemingly at random, as if hoping to bore or lose their followers.

Goby was playing this game one day. He was on edge, checking for small predators, who would be along soon in search of egg sacs to devour. One by one, his friends turned back as the original Silversides and his oldest nursling went further afield. Finally, Goby realized only he was left, and he was so far back he doubted Silversides even knew he was there.

To be sure of it, he kept to whatever cover the shadows and rocks and plants provided, and he kept on Silversides' trail. Because, once their playful escort had tired of the sport, the Silversides headed straight for the island where Goby had left his two-legs.

He couldn't see them now, but followed them by the faint, indefinable trace in the water by which the pod kept track of one another, almost dissipated at this distance.

They skirted the island's small sandy beach, a notch in an otherwise unapproachable coast. He thought they were going beyond the island, but suddenly he lost their track.

Goby turned back and swam closer to the island. *There!* The trace picked up and grew stronger as he neared the rocky shoreline, led him down and into a tunnel in the rocks not far from the sea bottom. He followed it as it slanted up. The water pressure lightened as he neared the surface; with a whispery splash, his head surfaced.

The tunnel opened into a cavern, its floor covered by little more than a film of sea water. There was light ahead. A breeze circulated in the cavern, bringing with it the sound of up-talk — the vocal language merfolk used out of water.

Goby awkwardly balanced himself on his long fluked tail and slithered forward, hoping the wavelets he made wouldn't alert the Silversides to his presence.

"—deep enough and more," the elder Silversides was saying. "I keep these shells to dip the sea water from the tunnel and carry it here several times a day, so the pit is always filled."

"Well-shaded," the younger Silversides said. "Secure, but. . . ."

"Utterly secure," the older Silversides said. "So now you know the first part of my secret. Here is where I always deposit my clutch."

No wonder no one ever saw him during spawning season! He was far from the pod, *on land*, keeping watch over his egg mass instead of dropping it and going about his everyday life like everyone else. And this was not just a one-year aberration; this was an annual obsession: an ongoing concentration on his own eggs that was so unnatural it was almost past understanding.

"And. . . ," young Silversides said, ". . . and I'm to do this, too?"

"No," the elder Silversides assured him. "This is for me."

"Ah. Well." The alarm in young Silversides' voice dropped to disinterest when the subject no longer concerned himself. "You said you'd show me where to deposit *my* eggs."

"Anywhere but here," the older voice said. "There. Or there. Anywhere out there."

". . .But. . . . I can't drop my eggs on land or in fresh water. Certainly not out there, in the sunlight. And not in this private place. They'd never get fertilized."

"That's the idea." The older Silversides hissed in frustration. "You are not to reproduce, don't you see? As long as I produce eggs, only mine are to be fertilized. Only mine are to hatch. And now, *two* of mine are to be nurtured — one by me and one by you. And next year, when your next younger nursemate is old enough, *three* of mine."

Goby had never heard anything so twisted. Like any other creature, he felt driven to take part in continuing the strength of the pod, in taking his chances in the great gamble of reproduction. But once he'd carefully placed his eggs or broadcast his sperm in the breeding grounds, his interest would end unless he took an urge to nurture.

Young Silversides' mind seemed to have swum the same stream, because he said, "What if I'm not ready to nurture this year?"

"It doesn't matter. All I need is your pouch to hold one of my young. I intend to take all responsibility for him. I want him to imprint on *me* as his nurshen. Always on me."

"And . . . and when I want to nurse a tad myself—"

"No. Only mine."

There was silence while young Silversides digested this.

The older voice said, "You haven't asked me the most important question yet. Have you guessed my biggest secret?"

After a moment, the younger mermayd asked the question Goby's age-mates had already asked each other about Silversides: "Who fertilizes the eggs?"

"I do! That's my biggest secret. I produce eggs and sperm in the same cycle and fertilize my own eggs and nurture my own tads. You'll all help me, one by one as your bodies are old enough, until I'm surrounded by myself. Until the entire pod is Silversides!"

Goby waited for the young Silversides to object — to reject this perversion of nature. He pressed himself against the cavern wall, listening. . . .

"Gotcha!" Grunion pounced on Goby's tail. "What are you doing way out here?"

Goby snatched his young nursemate up and threw himself headlong back toward the tunnel, using the momentum to slide across the wet floor.

Webbed hands grasped his flukes and he jerked to a painful halt. He should have released Grunion, should have shouted to him to swim for help, but instinct betrayed him and he clutched the young one rather than let him go careening away. The Silversides pulled and shoved the nursemates into the outer cavern, past the older Silversides' egg pit and onto a ledge above a freshwater pool. Nictating membranes snicked over their eyes, protecting their vision from the harsh sunlight and turning the world to shades of gray.

The older Silversides wrenched Grunion from Goby's arms and held him over the drop.

"Be still! Be still, or I let him go!"

Goby froze in place. "Give him to me."

"No. Be quiet. Let me think."

Young Silversides held Goby's wrists tightly.

The older mermayd seemed to speak to Grunion, as he said, "This is my secret. No one else must ever know about it."

Grunion, not too young to recognize danger, squeaked, "I can keep a secret. I promise."

"Can you?"

"I really can. I'd prove it to you, but I can't tell any secrets I know or they wouldn't be secrets anymore."

The older Silversides chuckled. "Clever tad."

"I can keep a secret, too," Goby said, though the thought of keeping this private sickened him. It was like knowing where an octopus lurked and not warning the pod.

"Can you?" the older Silversides said again. "Do you swear? If I promise to give you back your nursemate, do you swear?"

Choking on it, Goby said, "I swear."

"And do you. . . ." He smiled, and tentacles of fear touched Goby's spine. "Do you swear to come back here at hatching time and take one of my hatchlings into your nurture pouch and stay with me until the tad is ready to take his place at my side? And do you promise to do it every year, as long as you can nurture?"

Goby couldn't answer at once. The horror of what was being asked, the impossibility of refusing with Grunion's life at stake, paralyzed his voice.

"You don't promise. I can see you don't. Ah, well."

The older Silversides released Grunion, who squealed as he fell, with a splash, into the unsupportive fresh water.

With a bellow worthy of a walrus, Goby tore himself free of young Silversides' grip and threw himself at the older mermayd. They struggled on the ledge, arms interlocked, tails writhing, trying to gain purchase on the slippery stone and against each other. Silversides was bigger and more powerful, and his tail had a full adult's length and muscle, but Goby was powered by rage and terror.

The older mermayd yanked one of Goby's braids, pulling him off-balance, and slammed his head against the floor. Goby jabbed a knuckle upward and caught Silversides just under the eye.

He only had a second's breathing space, then both Silversides converged on him at once.

In a welter of thrashing arms and tails, all three rolled over the edge and crashed into the pool below.

Grunion! Goby's gills drew in the unwholesome fresh water, finding only traces of the richness a sea creature needed to survive. The tad was so young—Goby couldn't remember, in his flash of panic, if Grunion was old enough to have functioning lungs yet. If he could find him . . . if he could get him out of the pool . . . would his nursemate have a chance to escape over land?

The fall had separated the three combatants, and Goby dove deep into the pool to search from the bottom up for his nursemate. *If he only missed the rocks. . . . If he only didn't hit too hard. . . .*

There! The limp little body hovered among the stems of the water plants, sunk in the less buoyant salt-free liquid. As Goby neared, Grunion's eyes opened, a puzzled look in them, and his lips parted. A series of bubbles floated upward, and Goby laughed. *Air bubbles! Functioning lungs!*

"Goby. . . ," Grunion gasped. "Something wrong wi' th's water. . . ."

Goby scooped him up and shot to the surface at an angle toward the pool's rocky edge. He tossed his nursemate onto the land, saying, "Go!"

"Go where?" Grunion wailed.

Goby turned to face the Silversides as they surfaced and streaked toward him. As he did, his eye was drawn to a movement on the shore: a figure with hair on its face and chin, that crouched on the rocks and that rose onto two tails.

"Hi! Hi!" Goby called, waving his arms as the two-tails had done at its departing shell. "Heer! Heer!"

Then the Silversides were upon him, one grappling at him and the other trying to land himself and go after Grunion.

They pressed him toward the low bank where, to his dismay, he could hear Grunion cheering for him.

A shower of dirt sprayed over his back and into the eyes of his opponents. They dove, letting the water clear their vision.

He took the opportunity to turn, and ducked in time to avoid a second shower. Grunion was doing his best to adapt the tail-flip of his shark-bashing lesson to land, scooping rocks and grit through the thinness of air.

"Grunion — go!" he shouted. "Go overland! You can do it! Get back to the—"

Again, his braid was jerked painfully, snapping his upper body back, forcing his eyes up toward the burning sun. He felt one of the Silversides slide past him while the other towed him away from the pool's rim and Grunion.

He heard unidentifiable sounds from the pool's edge. What was Grunion up to now? Or was it the two-tails? If that creature did anything to hurt Grunion. . . .

The grip on his braid released and he rounded on his attacker, momentarily blinded by his protectively darkened eye membrane, and struck out at random. His fist connected with something hard, and his enemy grunted in surprise and pain.

Again blindly, he shoved the heels of both hands toward the source of the grunt and connected with what felt like a chin. With a flip of his tail, he sent himself racing toward Grunion.

"Oof!" He slammed into another body, driving it into the muddy rocks around the pool's edge.

A hand fastened around his wrist — the unoiled skin of it feeling like dry sand — and he was hoisted out of the water and onto the rocky edge. Grunion clasped his little arms around his neck.

In the shade of the overhanging trees, Goby's inner eyelids opened enough to show the two-tails, his tails — or lower arms or legs or whatever they were — braced apart from each other for better balance, throwing stones with impressive accuracy at the nearer Silversides. The more distant one, the elder, kept his distance and shouted alarms.

The younger one responded and joined his nurshen — and dam and sire — underwater.

Goby scooped Grunion up and held him tight until the tad wriggled for room.

"You all right, sprat?" he asked.

"I scraped my flukes. Is that a two-tails? Is it really?"

"Yes." Goby reached out and stroked the two-tails'

upper arm. "I saved its life. I think it's trying to show its gratitude."

Grunion reached out, too, and Goby held him close enough to touch the dry skin with a small finger.

"A real two-tails! Can we keep it?"

A webbed hand slapped the ground next to the two-tails' fluke, and the older Silversides tried to haul himself onto the bank, teeth bared in fury.

The two-tails balanced stiffly on one tail, bent the other one up, and brought it down on Silversides' hand. With a sharp cry, Silversides slipped back into the water.

Goby gave the two-tails a final approving pat and, Grunion nearly throttling him with excitement, slithered into the undergrowth, following a path no doubt worn by the two-tails between the pool and the beach where Goby had first left it.

~*~

He and Grunion returned to the pod, hurtling past sharks and age-mates alike, to find Manta and tell him what had happened. Manta gathered the other elders and they followed Goby back to the tunnel entrance, ordering him to wait for them there. When they came back out, the Silversides weren't with them.

"Couldn't they get back up on the ledge?" Goby asked. "I can lead you to the pool from the beach. The two-tails might stop throwing rocks at them if I tell it to, and they can come out the way Grunion and I did."

"It's too late," Manta said. "They were in the fresh water too long."

Goby felt sick. Life was dangerous — everybody knew that — but this was wrong. It was so bizarre. And it was his fault. They would still be alive, if he hadn't followed them. If he hadn't brought the two-tails to Silversides' secret place.

"It didn't mean to kill them," Goby said. "It didn't know any better."

Manta stroked his hair. "Nobody blames the animal," he said. "And nobody blames you. If they hadn't died before we got here, we would have killed them. The older one, anyway, for trying to kill you and Grunion *and* for . . . the rest of it. You had a lucky escape, and so did Grunion and so did all the Silversides nursemates. He would have stolen all their young for as long as he could, and the descendents of their young. The beast you saved didn't mean to, but it did the pod a favor."

~*~

So it was that the pod began keeping a two-person watch near the border of the upper and lower skies. One day, one of the two-tails' giant shells entered their waters again, and one of the watchers darted back to the pod to alert them. The other broke the surface, waving his arms and shouting the two-tails cry Goby had taught them all: "Hi! Hi! Heer! Heer!"

Two-tails crowded to the rim of the shell, pointing and making sounds at each other. One pointed a stick, and the watcher, having been told such a stick could shoot death, kept away until the stick was lowered.

Another mermayd surfaced farther off and gave the cry and the first one dove below.

The ship changed course to follow, as one member of the pod after another hailed it, leading it toward the island where Goby's two-tails was stranded.

Meanwhile, Goby raced to the island. His two-tails had fashioned a shelter just under the tree-line where it went to escape the worst of the sun. Goby called it out and pointed to sea.

It laughed and shouted as the shell came into view. Moving with surprising quickness on its two nearly rigid tails, it levered itself to the top of a stony hill, where it stretched high, waving its arms and calling out to its fellows.

Goby slipped back into the water. The other mermayds joined him for a triumphant return to the pod's territory.

Two-tails and their shells became more common in the area for a while, but they were easily avoided. The Silversides tads were taken in by other nurshen. They never really fit in with the pod, but their debased line was soon scattered in the wholesome impersonal reproductive process that was natural to the highest species.

Out of the Cradle

I learned my lesson about the land when I was not much bigger than these youngsters. I had only hatched four months earlier and was barely swimming on my own, but I thought I knew as much as any of the grown merfolk.

"Stay away from the beach!" the old ones warned us, over and over, and we paid as little attention as these youngsters do now.

I hear myself echoing the cry I scoffed at when I was just a tad: "Stay away from the beach!" I dart between the mertads and the treacherous land, and slap my tail on the water's surface.

I ought to let them take their chances, but I'm always more protective if I've happened to be there when the tads hatch, as I was with these. I worry more, and do more than my share of the minding. The stress makes me feel older than my seven years. Every day, I find more white hairs on my head and more silver scales on my tail. Sometimes I wonder if it's worth the trouble — but I know it is. When I see mertads playing, leaping free of the ocean, grasping at one another's hands or fins, their hair streaming behind them, I could weep for joy.

. . .And I order them back to the deeps.

The day I was telling about, the day I learned how little I knew, I had just turned four months, so I would have been about the size of an old one's palm.

It was a day when the upper sky sprayed its weird, flavorless water into the rich broth of the lower sky, the sea. Waves were high. Everyone over three months old played in the whitecaps, letting the swells lift them and then sliding into the wave troughs. Parents patrolled the deeps, guarding against predators — sharks and rays who love nothing more than a quick snack of merfolk too young to give them trouble.

I had been warned many times to stay clear of the strand, but I was sure my elders were just timid or dull or stupid, or were mindlessly repeating meaningless nonsense just because they had been told it when they were young. I could see the water roll onto the shore, then drag out to sea. It looked like it would be tremendous fun to ride a wave in and back — and absolutely safe.

I rode in, but my expected easy landing was a savage *thump!* The air was forced from every bladder in my body and I was left gasping on the damp sand. Panicked, I thrashed and flopped, and felt myself fall blissfully into salt water.

But I was not in the ocean. I was in a tide pool, cut off from safety by a wall of rock. Worse, I was not alone. With me was one of our young's deadliest enemies — a crab. It was over twice my size as I was then, and I was completely at its mercy.

I cried for help but I was too far from the deeps for anyone to hear my tiny airborne voice, and no one could have come to me if they had heard.

The crab darted at me. I dodged, scooping sand from the bed of the tide pool with my tail and flicking it into its eyes. That slowed it down for a few seconds, but there was nowhere for me to swim, nowhere to hide, no way to escape. All I could do was evade, with capture and death at the end. It lunged at me again, pincers snapping. I twisted away, but it caught me by the hair. I strained against its grip, but it was bigger and stronger than I was. With sickening ease, it drew me toward its mandibles, ready to rend me with its other claw and stuff the pieces into its foul belly.

An ear-splitting noise from above nearly drove the crab from my mind. A gigantic creature towered at the rim of the tide pool, blocking the sun. It had two extra arms where its tail should be. Its neck, where it should have had gills, was hideously smooth. It was the real-life monster the old ones use to frighten naughty tads — the Drylander!

It made another noise and scooped up the crab, with me still dangling by the hair from one pincer.

I had never seen a Drylander so close before, though the old ones always claimed the monsters could swim, and every old one knew somebody who knew somebody who had either drowned one or saved one's life.

This one turned the crab to get a better look at me, and my captive captor took the opportunity to nip the hand that held it.

With a roar, the Drylander flung the crab — with me still attached — out to sea. The two of us swam through the air over the heads of my spawnmates who had gathered thick as algae. As if in a dream, I watched the Drylander suck its wounded hand and dance on its lower arms.

We plunged into the ocean, and the deeps had never felt so good! I had hoped the crab would lose its grip on me when we hit, but my hair was tangled around its claw.

I cried out again. Now that I was undersea, the vibrations of my wail pierced the water and brought my mother and father. They were both young but full-grown, as much bigger than the crab as the crab was bigger than I.

So, instead of him making a meal of me, dinner went the other way around. My parents are very fond of crab, which saved me from punishment for my foolhardy disobedience.

That was the day I learned to believe the old ones' warnings—to stay out of the shallows and away from the land. But does it do me any good to tell my young ones that? I might as well be talking to the reef.

Blood of Mermayds

I heard the mermayds coming from halfway down the street, even with my restaurant's door closed. It sounded like a whole pod of them, which wasn't surprising — you didn't often see the younger ones alone on the land, and the older ones got that way by not attracting undue attention.

"Don't you open that door, Muriel," my cousin said. "They'll think they're welcome."

Mermayds didn't often have money, but I didn't mind bartering a meal for some fresh fish or seaweed, and I could always find a market for the odd pearl or such. My cousin Iris was older by ten years, and some would say I should have obeyed her. Still, it was my restaurant and she worked for me, so I opened the door.

There were three of them, taking up half the street, gliding over the cobbles with their long, muscular, fluked tails glistening, rippling behind them. Older ones usually wore tops that covered their featureless chests, disguising the evidence that they weren't mammals, but these tads were bare-chested. The two with dark hair wore high-quality gill-bands that would filter oxygen for them for up to two weeks, but the band on the blond tad was cheap and good for no more than a day. First time on land, was my guess.

They called back and forth in the clicking, squealing language they used to each other out of the water.

Iris looked past me and shuddered. "Ugh! Nasty things. Talking snakes, is what they are."

"People with tails," I said, just to be contrary.

"Uncle Phineas doesn't like them. You can see him staring at them in here and in the street."

"Uncle" Phineas was one of those new priests who claimed districts and demanded tithes. I thought they should call themselves something other than Uncle and Aunt, which is how the true priests of Micah title themselves. Iris can say mermayds on land are unnatural all she wants to, but I say a priest making demands is worse.

I pulled my wild black hair back and tied it at the nape of my neck with a bit of twine.

The blond one turned toward me at my movement, flailing for balance as it found itself whipping around with unexpected speed. New out of water, like I thought.

They all looked at me then. The black protective lenses that shielded mermayd eyes from straight sunlight gave them all an eerie look, I had to admit.

"Don't let them in," Iris said, already knowing I would.

The blond one recovered its balance, laughing along with the others, showing its teeth in what looked like a grimace, but passed for a smile with them.

After they traded some noise, the dark ones approached my door, the blond one behind them.

"I'm on break," Iris said, heading for the back door.

As they got closer, I recognized the dark ones, and even remembered the landfolk versions of their names.

"Jack. Skate." I mangled as close a version as I could manage of their greeting noises, and they laughed and returned it. "Who's your friend?"

They described the fish to me in much better land talk than my mer talk attempt, and I said, "Loach, I guess."

After a few more clicks, squeaks, whistles and practice tries, the blond tad had its first land words: Loach and Muriel.

I don't know why I took a personal interest in that one. Maybe because one of its first land words was my name. But the feeling seemed to go both ways: It dropped in to the restaurant every couple of weeks, tagging after Jack and Skate at first, then showing off by guiding other newlanders to "this place that accepts merfolk right through the front door". I had a table in the corner that they used; they pushed the benches back against the walls and sat on their coiled tails.

After a couple of months, I started thinking of Loach as "him" instead of "it", even though a mermayd might lay egg clumps or might fertilize egg clumps from one year to another, so there wasn't any "him" or "her" to them. He usually paid me with fish, lobsters, oysters, abalone, conch or some other edible.

It always made me nervous when Uncle Phineas and Loach were in my place at the same time. Iris was right: Phineas always looked at mermayds with that calculating stare he used whenever you wore a new cloak or put a new coat of paint on the walls, like he was wondering if it was time to raise your tithes.

One day, Phineas came in just as Loach and his friends were moving away from their table. At first, I thought somebody had shut the door, but then I saw it was the priest. He's 6'6" and he doesn't make up for his height by being skinny. He has to stoop and turn sideways to get through the small door I'd never bothered to enlarge when I turned the storehouse into a restaurant.

Phineas loomed over me as I hurried to greet him, hoping to distract his attention from the mermayds in the corner.

I could have saved myself the trouble. Instead of easing out, Loach made a point of coming to take formal leave of me — something he never did, by the way. He also proved how much he had learned about handling his bulk on land by raising himself, balancing on his coils, until he was just half an inch or so taller than Phineas.

The priest looked up, memorizing the tad's face. The corners of Uncle Phineas' mouth turned down in his particular version of a smile. It was not the kind that lit up a room.

"Out," I told Loach, concern making my voice harsh. "All three of you. Out. Now."

"See you again soon," he said.

The whole effect was rather spoiled by his having to lose half his height in order to get through the door. To move at all, for that matter.

I got the feeling Uncle Phineas was amused but, to give him credit, he didn't laugh.

He sat at his usual table and nodded when I asked if he wanted his usual order. He loved my lobster chowder and the beer I brewed in the cellar. I got a break on my temple dues in exchange for never bringing him a bill when he deigned to grace my wharf-rat chow-house with his custom.

When I brought his food and drink, he flicked a finger toward my bracelet and said, "A gift from your mermayd friend?"

"I made it out of copper wire and red coral. One of the mermayds traded it to me for a month of meals." It had been

Loach who did the trade, but I wasn't about to give his name.

"Do you know what they call red coral? 'Blood of Mermayds'. People used to think that's what red coral was. More precious as jewelry than as life fluid."

"Depends on whether you're a mermayd or not," I said.

Iris, who, as usual, had come back when she saw the mermayds leave, bustled up and wiped a non-existent spill from the table.

"You shouldn't make jokes like that," she scolded me. "The Uncle doesn't know you're playing." She pushed the salt cellar closer to Phineas' hand. "Muriel's a businesswoman," she said. "If she can get value from mermayd trade, she takes it. Maybe serving them in the restaurant is going too far, but I can't argue with reasonable profit."

"Indeed," said the priest. "Who could?"

Iris and I tugged each other away from the table, she being afraid I'd offend the Uncle with inappropriate friendships, I being afraid she'd press the profit angle until he raised my tithes.

He lifted a hand and we froze in place. A flick of his fingers called me back.

"I've had a letter from a colleague in Barria. He reminded me of a dish I enjoyed when I visited him last: the eggs of a sturgeon. That's a kind of fish they have in the deep waters there."

I had never heard of that fish. I had heard of Barria, of course. Anybody with a business around the coast knew about various ports of call. I had even heard of fish eggs. I put them on the menu, when they turned up. Mermayds loved them. So did Uncle Phineas.

"I'll send word, the next time I open a fish with eggs in it."

"I fancy sturgeon eggs. Fresh."

"But how. . . ."

His mouth turned down in what passed for his smile as he saw that I understood. "I would consider it a personal favor," he said.

The next time Loach was in, I asked him.

"Female sturgeon, ready to spawn," he said. "I'll pass the word and see what I can do."

A few days later, some of Loach's younger friends were in without him.

"He's away," one of them said. "Seems it's spawning season for sturgeon, and he and Jack and Skate went to bring back a few. One to tow the bag net and two to guard against shark and so on."

I hadn't thought of the danger. I hadn't thought of anything except staying on Phineas' good side.

But another week went by, and Loach, Jack and Skate turned up at the back door, safe and sound, lugging a six-foot burlap sack soaked with sea water between them.

They got it in and unwrapped it on my prep table. Almost six feet of silver from tip to tail, the iridescence of life was still just fading from it.

"She's been opened." The slit in her belly gaped as I prodded her.

"Sure," Loach said. "Heavy enough, without the guts. Did you want the guts, or just the fish and the eggs? Besides, I had to make sure she was carrying, didn't I?"

I checked. Carefully.

"Perfect!" I got a precious little bowl — a gift from a sailor friend — made of real molded glass. Using a wooden spoon, I eased the tiny black eggs into the bowl. They didn't look appealing to me. The fish eggs we get around here tend to be golden or orange, not this nasty black.

"Thank you!" I said it again, or as close as I could come, in sea talk. "I owe you for this."

The mermayds waved away my thanks with hisses of laughter. "It was fun," Loach said.

As the door closed behind them, I called for Iris and Alder.

Fish eggs generally kept a couple of weeks in a coldroom, if they didn't get eaten first, but I hoped to have this treasure out of my shop and into my favor-to-a-priest account sooner than that.

"Iris, I need help in here. Alder, run and tell Uncle Phineas I have his special order. Ask when he wants it. Then tell Simeon I need him now. Then spread the word we have a foreign fish called sturgeon, and plenty of it. I don't want any of this to go to waste."

By the time Alder came back with word that Uncle Phineas wanted his treat delivered to his personal quarters in his temple, Simeon had the sturgeon cut into steaks and chunks, simmering in chowder, skewered for kabobs, marinating in three different brews, and rubbed with dry spices. Iris and I had chopped onions, boiled chicken eggs, fried and crumbled bacon, toasted thin-sliced bread, and prepared all the side bits that Uncle Phineas favored with fish eggs.

Iris, always ready to curry favor with the clergy, volunteered to carry the basket to Phineas, but I didn't trust her not to stop and brag and show the special dish to her cronies. So I scrubbed down with lemon soap, put on a fresh dress, tied back my hair and slipped out the back.

Uncle Phineas' temple wasn't far from the wharfs, but the distance was more than just distance. It had begun as a fortress, carved out of the rock of a promontory commanding a full view of the harbor. He'd built on that, and now he had a minor castle, with enough windows to oversee everything. Some of the windows reflected the sun from real glass covering.

A wide, gentle slope led from the street to the temple. The kind of folk who had gone to Phineas' temple — in the time before we were all forced to attend — didn't like to strain themselves. His private quarters were off to the side, up another slope, its entrance inside a courtyard.

Several of the new style of churchwarden, the kind with helmets and knives and truncheons, lounged in the courtyard, looking both relaxed and menacing. I tried to look like I wasn't intimidated.

"He's expecting me. I'm Muriel, with his lunch."

I knocked, and his sexton, an overfed scavenger named Reynold, let me in. He didn't like it when Phineas dismissed him to his duties, but he cast a routinely suspicious look at me and took his pushiness elsewhere.

Phineas settled himself in a padded chair near a window with a view of the harbor and had me set up a scribe's desk for him. I unpacked the dishes and arranged them the way he liked them: empty plate in front of him, chopped eggs, minced onion, sliced lemon, and thin-sliced toast in a semi-circle around it. Finally, I unpacked the cooler of salted ice with the little glass pot of eggs and the little wooden spoon for dipping the eggs out. I unscrewed the lid of the pot and set the cooler at the top of the semi-circle.

Phineas stopped rubbing his hands together and leaned forward.

I leaned forward, too. It looked just like it had when I'd packed it: a mass of tiny black eggs, shiny and unbroken. "What is it? What's wrong?"

He sat back and gave me that calculating stare of his.

"How did you come by these?"

"I told one of the mermayds I wanted some, and he and some friends went and fetched some sturgeon. They brought me one with these in it."

"Whole? The fish was intact and alive?"

"Well. . . . No. He had opened it to clean it and to make sure these were there."

The corners of his mouth turned down. "I see."

I saw, too. "These aren't sturgeon eggs, are they?"

He shook his head, his mouth being full of toast, eggs, fish eggs and onion.

"He switched them on me. Kept the sturgeon eggs for himself and put these in their place."

Phineas nodded, chewing with relish.

"Are they any good, anyway?"

He swallowed and said, "Quite good, actually. Beautifully fresh, and perfectly handled. Not, however, sturgeon."

I ground my teeth so hard they squeaked. Iris had been right about not trusting mermayds. If anything could be worse than disappointing one of these new priests — particularly Uncle Phineas — it was having to give Iris credit for being right.

"Indulge my curiosity." Phineas shoveled another spoonful of egg and onion onto toast and balanced a dollop of the small black fish eggs on top. "Which mermayd supplied this?"

The name was in my mouth. My tongue had positioned

itself for the "L", but I couldn't do it. I couldn't aim Uncle Phineas at Loach and loose the arrow.

"Who can tell them apart?" Besides, this was a betrayal I wanted to deal with myself. "I'll send you some grilled sturgeon for your supper. And I'll have some fresh mushrooms I was going to make into a soup, but I'll fry them up in double-cream butter just for you. And some nice, fresh cress. And I'll see if they brought any more sturgeon. If they did, and it's still alive, I'll dress it myself and bring you the eggs tomorrow."

"You don't know who it was, or you won't tell me?" He wiped his hands and mouth on his priestly green napkin and pinned me with his stare.

Speechless, I could only shake my head *No*.

He grunted. "Very well. I look forward to that supper. You need not bring it yourself, but I prefer to be spared Iris."

"Yes, Uncle Phineas."

"And let me know if you'll have the sturgeon eggs for me tomorrow."

"Yes, Uncle Phineas."

"You may go. I'll send someone with your things."

"Yes Uncle Phineas."

As I reached the door, he said, "And send Joel to me."

In the blessed fresh air and sunshine, I told the wardens, "He wants Joel," and hurried back to the restaurant.

I stuck my head in the front door, making sure my quarry wasn't there. He was brazen enough for that. There were no mermayds in the place, though, so I threaded the streets leading to the harbor.

I saw a few mermayds, but nobody I recognized, and there was no use asking them anything. Except with people they knew, they usually pretended not to understand land talk.

The closer I got to the harbor, the more mermayds mingled with the landfolk, although the sea people were still far in the minority. Every so often, I even saw one alone, though the solitary ones looked wary and invariably had at least one knife strapped on where it was easily drawn.

I turned a corner, and there he was, just coming out of an all-goods shop, his webbed hands unrolling a high-quality gillband for close inspection.

He was so intent on it, he didn't see me until I snatched the band and clutched it in a shaking fist.

"This is *mine*, I think."

"What—"

"You bought it with my money. Good coin I paid you for sturgeon eggs, which I did not get!"

He hissed laughter, showing sharp teeth, holding his hands in front of himself, pantomiming a mockery of self-defense.

"Do you think it's funny? I should have told him who deceived me. Thank Micah he believed it, when I told him I brought them to him in good faith."

"You wanted them for a customer?" Loach seemed to think this was funnier than ever. "What did he say? He knew they weren't the real thing?"

"Of course he did! Is there anything he *doesn't*?"

"Who? Who was it? Anyone I would know?"

"Oh, you tell me. Do you know Uncle Phineas?"

The laughter melted from his face like wet paint in the rain. When he spoke again, it was with the stilted pronunciation of one new to land talk.

"You didn't tell me they were for him. I wouldn't have

done that to you. I swear!"

"You swear! What good is the word of a mermayd?"

"I can make it right! We brought back more than one sturgeon. I still have one alive. You can have it. All of it. Send your man for it and he can haul her up alive. You can open her, yourself."

His expression changed again, and his gaze focused beyond me.

I turned and saw a churchwarden, armored in black, caped, armed, helmeted and veiled, watching us from the corner. Was this the "Joel" Uncle Phineas had sent for? Was this why he had called for him? To send him after me so I could lead him to my swindler?

"What are *you* looking at?" I spoke more harshly to the warden than perhaps I should, but I didn't like being spied on.

"I'm not sure," a masculine voice said. "Am I looking at a mermayd who thinks it's funny to play jokes on land folk? On priests?" One hand rested comfortably on the handle of his truncheon.

Behind me, I heard Loach gasp, the gillband he wore unable to compensate for his panic.

"Who, this one?" I turned around and handed Loach his new purchase. "He was just showing me his latest pretty."

The warden approached us slowly, and I felt him scrutinizing both of us, memorizing us from top to toe — or tailtip.

The last voice I wanted to hear sounded from the corner, where the warden had been. And, when I say "the last voice I wanted to hear", remember that that includes Iris' and Uncle Phineas'.

Uncle Phineas' sexton, Reynold, said, "It doesn't matter if this is the one or not. One of them played the fool with a priest. Punish one, send a message to them all."

"What message would that send them? That land folk are stupid?" I walked toward Reynold, throwing an arm over maybe-Joel's shoulder as I passed and drawing him along with me. Over my shoulder, I clicked and hissed, "Go. Be at that place with that thing," which was as good as I could do on the spur of the moment.

Reynold said, "I didn't give it permission to leave."

I drowned him out with a jovial, "Uncle Phineas and I have arrangements all made. It's all taken care of. Now, why don't the two of you come back to my place and have a couple of beers and a dish or two of oysters on the house?"

Reynold, peevish, repeated, "I didn't give it permission to leave."

"I'm sorry. I thought you said, 'Permission to leave.'" A glance behind us showed a total absence of Loach. "I beg your pardon," I said, stopping. "Should I call him back?"

Reynold's face attempted Uncle Phineas' calculating stare but only looked constipated. "It's gone."

"They certainly can move fast, when they want to," I said. "Now let me get you two some beer and oysters. It was only a mermayd, right? Nothing to get upset about."

I led the way back to my place, gave orders to Simeon for retrieving what had better be a real sturgeon really full of real sturgeon eggs, and invested a large plate of oysters and two tankards of beer in improving my relations with the clergy.

I wished I thought it was money well spent.

Becalmed At Sea

Deep below the water's surface, the two mermayds left the current they had been following and regarded the keel of the small boat above them.

Marlin, the one with red hair, said, in the high, rapid underwater speech of the mermayds, "What's a boat that small doing this far off shore? They must have been caught in that storm on the coast yesterday."

Blennie, criss-crossed with puckered red scars from neck to fluke, and with eyes small, sunken, and weak, said, "Who cares?"

Marlin joggled Blennie's elbow. "You care. Let's go see if they need help."

"I thought we were in a hurry for the gathering."

"So let's hurry." Marlin shoved at the water with his long, powerful tail. When he saw his companion hadn't moved, he looked back.

Blennie hugged his own damaged chest and called, "Stay out of harpoon range."

Marlin returned — safely — and reported, "I was right. They were heading up the coast when that storm blew out and grabbed them. If we can get them a wee bit east, they can catch the evening exhalation and make land. Maybe not where they really *meant* to land, but land."

"Their problem is not our problem."

Marlin didn't argue. He had raised more tads than most mermayds, and knew better than to try to reason with that sullen obstinacy. Not that Marlin's friend was a tad, but the mistreatment Blennie had suffered at the hands of two landwalkers had turned him in on himself.

"I'm going to see if enough of the others will help turn and tow the boat," Marlin said. "I'd like it if you stayed here so we can find it without getting cricks in our necks from looking up for it. Or you can come along and stay at the gathering once we get there."

Blennie wanted to leave the boat's occupants behind and forget they existed, but Marlin had taken him in after the . . . incident, and deserved better.

"I'll stay," he said.

"I'll be quick." Before the last echoes of his words had faded from Blennie's ears, Marlin was out of sight.

Blennie floated in place, flicking a webbed hand or a fluke now and then to counteract a pressure fluctuation.

After one such correction, a realization akin to joy flooded him: He could follow Marlin and tell him a breeze had come up and the boat had sailed away. By the time the gathering was over, the humans would all be dead.

He imagined the two-tails, sunscorched and desiccated, all their juices sucked dry by the treacherous air.

He shuddered in horror and shame. Only two landwalkers had hurt him. Others had rescued him, and still others had given him safe passage back to the sea. Still, those two weren't alone in their hatefulness.

Before he could decide what to do, much sooner than he expected, Marlin returned with six others, all former nurselings of Marlin's.

"They were coming out to meet us," he said, and Blennie knew, whether Marlin did or not, that it wasn't Blennie they were coming out to meet.

He still refused to help, but the seven easily turned the boat and towed it to where it picked up a breeze it could tack into and ride to safety.

Marlin and his nurselings surrounded Blennie when they returned, included him, swept him along with them to the gathering, gracing him with all the marks and behaviors that said he was equal family.

Blennie hoped Marlin didn't suspect the temptation he hadn't resisted but only outlasted. It wouldn't have surprised him, though, to learn that hope was vain.

Alien Earth

Science fiction isn't always about outer space, of course; it can be set right here on Earth.

The first two stories in this section are what I call "soft steampunk". True, classic steampunk is a form of alternate history in which inventions of modern times were invented in the past, but worked by steam or clockwork; the "punk" part comes from a dystopian component, with a strong thread of anti-establishmentarianism. Soft steampunk is a travesty, and, of course, that's what I write: steam, clockwork, blimps, sky pirates, and nonsense are my watchwords. Any social consciousness is purely coincidental. So, no, I don't consider myself a steampunk author; I just play one in my own mind sometimes.

"Dog Star" is a good old alien crash-landing on Earth story, told from the point-of-view of the dogs who find him. "Sure Thing" is a flash fiction buddy story in which one of the buddies is an earthling and one is his alien hired hand.

"Pile-up" posits a scientific understanding that we haven't yet reached, but that I'm ready for when it comes.

"Snow on the Screen" . . . Not quite sure what to say about that one.

The rest of the pieces in this section take place in Earth's future.

SMILE, Mr. President

The annual convention of the Steam Motorcar Inventors' League of England (North American Division) had never been so gloomy.

Her Majesty, Queen Victoria, had spoken and written so strongly against the pollution of coal-burning vehicles that public sentiment had turned against it. Parliament was debating – and would probably pass — laws against internal combustion conveyances.

Sir Beauregard Beanblossom expressed the bitterness of them all when he said, "Folks can still burn coal in their fireplaces and kitchen stoves, oh, yes. Businesses can still belch out volcanoes'-worth of cinders and clinkers, but motorcars? Oooo, nasty!"

Ms. Daisy Lee sniffed and said, "Just because Her Majesty got a bit of something in her eye the last time she took a train, nobody can run a vehicle on coal anymore. It's back to the horse-and-buggy days for the entire world."

The familiar lament was interrupted by the entrance of the League's youngest member.

Membership in the League was difficult to earn, but young Theodore Roosevelt's energy and penetrating insight had won him a place with a speed that some of the more plodding members resented.

Roosevelt was accompanied by four hotel footmen. Two of them cleared a demonstration table and made sure its thick cork cover was firmly in place. The other two tried, vainly, to take Roosevelt's boxed armful from him and carry it (which was, after all, one of their jobs). Roosevelt thanked them and declined, winning the dispute as he lowered his burden with a thud that spoke of its weight.

In his surprisingly high-pitched voice, he said, "Ladies and gentlemen, I give you my latest invention: a new kind of steam engine, *that does not burn coal!*"

He undid a latch on the lid of the box and folded down the sides. The engine he revealed looked almost identical to any other; the greatest visible difference was a pipe that seemed to pass through something that looked like a lady's winter hand muff. A net the size of a man's head was affixed to the back of the final length of pipe.

Roosevelt filled the radiator with water supplied by one of the footmen. With a flourish, he drew a roughly cylindrical object from his pocket and fed it into the firebox. He pressed the spark switch several times before his fuel caught fire, which was not unusual: getting the machine going was generally the hardest part of running one.

He added no coal. He added nothing.

A small explosion inside the firebox sent some members diving under tables.

"Nothing to be afraid of," Roosevelt called to them. "That's what it does. Perfectly safe." He, himself, stood next to the machine without flinching. Although the other League members knew Roosevelt would stand next to the machine even if he knew it might go off like a bomb, they re-seated themselves and attempted not to fidget.

Another small explosion. Another. Then, more and more quickly, more and more explosions. With each one, the pistons moved the rods, faster and faster, until Roosevelt adjusted the throttle to control the speed. From the smokestack came a thin black smoke and only the finest ash. From the back of the new pipe array shot small white irregular globes. The smell was divine.

"Popcorn!" Sir Beauregard pounded the table. "Popcorn, by Fulton!"

"I only attached the net to save Housekeeping the chore of sweeping it up," said Roosevelt. "On the road, the popped kernels can simply scatter and be eaten by birds or allowed to go back to nature. For use in the cities, I plan to add an attachment that will use part of the energy generated to grind the popped kernels as they exit the firebox, to collect in bricks suitable for burning in the home."

The rest of the convention was spent in studying Roosevelt's invention, assembling another model from his parts and plans, arguing violently but happily over improvements and refinements, sketching applications, and drafting a letter to Parliament begging them to allow SMILE to present them with this new apparatus before they passed their conveyance law.

If Parliament approved, SMILE would hasten forward quickly to produce a prototype popcar.

Everyone agreed that young Theodore would be president of SMILE someday. President Roosevelt. It had a ring to it.

Three Men in a Blimp, To Say Nothing of the Automaton

There was this chap named Jay and two other chaps whose names I forget, and they took their dog with them and went a bit of a way up the Thames in a rowboat, and the chap named Jay wrote about it, and everybody in England went mad over it, and everybody who could scrape up two friends and a dog tried the same thing.

So the three of us: Morris (Minor) Applethwaite, Bernard (Conkers) Conklin, and I, William Whimsey (they call me Old Bill), decided we wanted to get in on the fun.

Conkers, of course, had to object. It isn't that he's an objectionable sort of fish, is Conkers; he just likes to be different. As a general rule, he's one of the most agreeable fellows I know. Third most agreeable, I'd say. No, I tell a lie: he's the fourth most agreeable. I was forgetting Jonas Crabtree, the tobacconist on the corner. Not your corner, of course, but my corner. Well, of course, it may be your corner, as well; I don't know where you live, after all, do I? No, I tell you quite frankly, I do not.

At any rate, Conkers said, "Look here, why should we do what everybody else is doing?"

"Because, you mutton-headed booby," said Minor, who tended to be brusque when thwarted, "everybody else is doing it. That's rather the point, isn't it?"

You may have noticed that I stayed out of it. I'm an observer of human nature. I was born that way, I suppose. They tell me I didn't even speak for the better part of the first three years of my life, I was so absorbed in observation. I'd still rather watch than participate, especially in work.

At any rate, I was busily observing Minor and Conkers eying one another with a wary willingness to come to blows if no better entertainment offered itself, when Conkers made his brilliant (he does have these flashes of brilliance sometimes, like lightning in a thick cloud) — I forgot where I was. Oh, yes, Conkers made his brilliant suggestion.

"Why don't we do the same thing, only different? Why don't we travel the route by balloon?"

Minor gave a rather unattractive snort of laughter. Minor fancies himself a bitter, saturnine man of the world, master of sarcastic wit.

"A balloon? A balloon, you poor lunatic?"

I thought it was high time I dove in and straightened out the conversation. It often falls to me to do so. It hardly seems fair that one out of three should always be the voice of sweet reason, but there it is. I like to think I bear the burden gracefully.

"Yes, you unmitigated ass," I said, "a balloon! A dirigible! A blimp! An airship, you fool!"

Minor's jaw dropped at the beauty of the thought. "Where would we get one?"

Conkers said, "We would rent one, you know."

"Who would fly it?"

"Old Bill would," said Conkers.

"Old Bill?" The disbelief in Minor's voice would have hurt me deeply, if I hadn't said the same thing at the same time in the same tone.

"Of course!" Conkers looked at the two of us as if we were idiots. "Old Bill can drive a steamcar without putting it into the ditch above twice in ten miles. If he can do that, it should be child's play for him to drive something that doesn't need a road."

Minor and I were much struck by the simple good sense of Conkers' logic.

I clapped my hands together and rubbed them in anticipatory glee. "Well, then," I said. "All we need now is a dog."

Minor tapped out his pipe tobacco in the fire (he knows I hate that), and said, "Must it be a terrier?"

The three men in a boat had a terrier, you see.

"I could borrow my Aunt Louisa's terrier," I said.

Minor recovered his habitual scorn. "A terrier in an airship? As mad as terriers are for jumping about?"

"My Aunt Louisa's terrier is an irritating dog," I said, thoughtfully. "Not to put too fine a point upon it—"

"Murder your aunt's dog on your own time," said Minor, rather ungenerously, I thought. "If we were to murder every irritating terrier we came across, we'd never do anything else. We won't take a terrier."

"What, then? Do you have a dog in mind?"

That was when Conkers had his second flash of brilliance in one evening. "We could buy a clockwork one. I saw one at the second-hand shop, the last time I pawned my watch."

"Did you, by Jove," said I.

"It isn't in the best shape, but I tried it, and it does work, after a fashion."

Minor had to quibble over trifles: "What sort of a dog is

it made to be?"

"The chap claimed it was meant to be a Cavalier King Charles Spaniel."

"Oh," said Minor, pacified. "Cheerful little dogs. Right-o!"

So we were agreed. We would rent a small airship and we would take a clockwork dog.

~*~

The provisions were simple. Although the three men in the boat took along a portable cooker and all manner of nonsense, we would take bread, apples, cheese (of the mildest odor obtainable), and a large flask of hot tea. We wouldn't want to sleep in the air, of course, so we would sink with the sun — land in the evening, I mean to say, you know — and take rooms. We would find a good local pub and have some simple fare and as much beer as we could hold. Unlike the poor blighters on the river, we could go inland and avoid the crowd and the price gouging.

Brilliant!

~*~

The day of our trip dawned, and we found our bespoke conveyance ready and waiting when we pulled up in my steamcar. As soon as Minor and Conkers had released their grips on whatever bits of the 'car they had clutched during the ride, we transferred our clothes boxes and hamper from the boot of the 'car into the airship's wickerwork gondola.

It wasn't overlarge, especially with the coal boxes, and it creaked alarmingly. It smelt distressingly of old straw, dry mold, and mechanical oil. The balloony bit loomed over the open basket.

Minor took exception to the openness, although we had discussed it earlier in relation to the propensity of terriers for jumping. No doubt he hadn't been listening. He seldom listens to anybody else, so it would hardly be implausible to suppose he didn't listen to himself, either. He would have far less profit in it if he did.

"I say," he growled, thrusting his chest out at the weedy little airship rental agent, "what do you mean by foisting this off onto us? Where are the bally windows? Where's the roof, eh? Do you expect us to go up and about in all winds and weathers with no protection? Eh?"

"Oh, 'scuse me, yer lor'ship," the man said with a sneer that could take first prize at any sneering contest anyone cared to sponsor, "I di'n't know money was no object."

Minor lost color at the mention of money changing hands. He harrumphed and turned away. "Very well, then," he said. "Let that be a lesson to you."

The man tipped me a wink and set about explaining the principles of inflating, deflating, fueling, and steering the contraption. Fairly simple, really: lightweight, semi-rigid envelope construction, blah-blah-blah, coal in here both heats the air in the envelope and powers the motors, umpty-umpty, propellers on each side in the rear, so-on-so-forth, rudder, etc.

We crossed his palm with the requisite silver, climbed in, donned the goggles he rented us for a small additional fee, waited for him to cast off (or whatever one calls untying the mooring rope and tossing it into the gondola), I fiddled with the appropriate thingummy, and we were off!

Ah! What could compare with the joy of that ascent? What a thrill, to watch the sad old world fall away beneath us, as if we were birds hitherto mired in the clinging mud of everyday toil and care, suddenly freed and soaring where our souls yearn to go and where our spirits precede us! Who among us has not longed to spread our wings and fly, rising above the grind of present circumstances to the very height of our ability and possibility? Who among us has not dreamed of it, waking or sleeping?

"Good Lord," Conkers shouted into my ear. "Nobody ever told me it would be so flaming LOUD!"

And it was loud, too, between the engines and the wind of our passage humming against the struts and ropes and the hot air exhausting up into the blimpy whatsit.

The tiresome chap who rented us the blimp had tried to insist that we forget about following the Thames and, instead, follow the coast south and west and around to Cornwall, where we could land at his cousin's shipyard, spend our holiday aground, and take the train back to London. I tried to explain to him that the whole point of the expedition was to spend our holiday in the air above the Thames, but he droned on about prevailing winds and half-wits being blown out to sea and brigands with their own airships and such rot as that. It does drive me so wild, when someone gabbles on and on about something of no earthly interest to me, doesn't it you?

I had to admit, though (to myself, of course; I wouldn't have admitted it aloud to those two jackanapes, even if they could have heard me over the noise), that I was having the devil of a time steering or making any headway. The bothersome machine would drift south, until we were moving with extreme slowness along the bank of the river, then parallel to the river, then within sight of the river. The farther south we drifted, the faster (or, rather, the less snail-like) we moved ahead, until we were following the coast, with Cornwall somewhere ahead.

~*~

We landed at Bognor Regis. The pier looked spiffing, lights

shining on the darkening water like so many acts of kindness in an unkind world. Conkers wanted to hare off and play skittles or some such foolishness, but Minor and I persuaded him — at full volume, to be heard over the engines and so on — that our money (what little the blimp man had left us) would be better spent on food and, more to the point, beer. We had just bumped to a landing that I still maintain was a good one at an all-night airship facility and were still luxuriating in the relative stillness when Minor said,

"I say, whatever became of that deuced dog? Don't tell me we've come off without him?"

"Oh!" said Conkers. "The dog! Yes, he's here, somewhere."

He rummaged around in the luggage, spilling a sack of buns and treading one underfoot, and came up with a rather shopworn pasteboard box with DOG scratched on it in pencil and, underneath this, "CAVALIER KING CHARLES SPANIEL??" Conkers broke the tape holding the box closed, opened the bent and dirty flaps, reached in, and removed an object roughly the size and general shape of a respectable loaf of bread.

He placed it on the floor of the gondola with the air of a cat who has caught something and presented it to you as a gift, though is having second thoughts about it even as he does so.

"If that's all it does," said Minor, "you might as well put it back in the box. I could *imagine* a better dog than that." Since everyone knows, and frequently states, that Minor has no imagination, I thought this statement a bit strong, and I could see by the look on Conkers' face that Conkers thought so, too.

"Wait a bit," Conkers said. "Let me wind him up and set him off, you know." He unfolded the beast's — or, I should say, the machine's — paws, tail, and head. My uncle Jasper had just such a dog, only a live one, if "live" is the word I want in connection with a creature so somnolent it didn't move even when we set off firecrackers next to it. Uncle Jasper moved, though, and so did we; he would never have caught us, if the butler, who was in league with him, hadn't locked the front door when we weren't looking.

At any rate, Conkers unfolded our dog, turned a screw in its belly, closed and latched the belly covering, and said, "Rex! Good! Boy!"

The thing quivered. Then, with a squeaking of rusty gears, it wove and wobbled to its feet, and the evening light fell full upon it. A Cavalier King Charles Spaniel, as you may know, has long, gently waved, silky hair and drooping ears, the hair generally being black on the body and white on the paws and legs. I am not, by nature, a skeptical man, and I was willing to stretch a point and concede the possibility that this pseudo-animal, in its prime, had been meant to resemble a Cavalier King Charles Spaniel. Now, though, its fur was tangled, matted, and, where it hadn't fallen out or been clipped off in order to remove something apparently even more repellent than the substances still adherent to it, a slightly greenish black and a more than somewhat grayish white. Its ears had been cut short, leaving flaps like those on the sides of deer-stalker hats to cover its earholes.

It lifted a front paw, turned its head toward Conkers, parted its flabby lips, and said, slowly, with a heavy grinding of its mechanism, "Argh! Argh!"

"Well," said Minor, "it isn't a terrier."

~*~

We didn't have the heart to leave Rex alone, and we didn't have the nerve to be seen with him, so we switched him off, put him back in the box, and took him with us.

Naturally, everybody in the pub wanted to know what we had in the box.

Isn't it always the way? If you have something that you just ache for people to ask you about — a spelling medal, say, or a newly published slim volume of one's own verses — nobody ever will. But just put a severed head in a hatbox or something, and people will stop you on the street to beg for a peek.

Minor, of course, got rather testy about it. Here's a typical interchange:

Stranger: Eh, what's in the box, an' all?

Minor: It's a dog.

Stranger: A dog? Devil it is! A dog?

Minor: Yes. No doubt even you have heard of them.

Stranger: Alive, is it? Or dead?

Minor: Look in the box and find out.

Sometimes they would, and sometimes they wouldn't. Of course, even then, they didn't know.

Conkers had another of his rare strokes of intelligence and began betting people a pint that they couldn't guess what it was.

A very successful evening, all in all.

~*~

We woke late the next morning in our room upstairs in the pub. Minor and I woke first, washed, dressed, shaved, and brought the polished boots in from the hall.

Together, we contemplated the revolting figure of Conkers, sprawled on his cot, drooling into his pillow, unshaven, uncleansed, unclothed (except, of course, for his nightshirt).

Minor turned from the hideous vision and opened the box. Using two handkerchiefs (Conkers' and, I found later, mine), he lifted Rex from the box, wound him up, put him on the cot next to Conkers, and switched him on.

"Rex! Wake him up!"

Rex came to his feet in a series of jerks. He stepped over the jumble of covers, tail-stump quivering. At Conkers' head, he pawed at the inert jaw. "Argh! Argh!" When Conkers didn't respond, Rex delighted us (Minor and me, I mean, not Conkers) by sticking his disintegrating rubber nose into Conkers' ear and releasing short puffs of air, giving the effect of snuffling (without, alas, the vital element of animal moistness).

The effect was all we could have hoped. Conkers bucked as if galvanized. Poor Rex flew off the bed and landed with a clank on the floor, where he spun in slow circles until I righted him with my socked foot.

"Good dog," I said.

Rex opened his jaws and unfurled a flannel tongue which appeared to have been used as a pen-wiper. "Argh! Argh!"

When Conkers finally ceased inventing new curses and had made himself as presentable as one could reasonably expect of him, we went downstairs to a bite of breakfast and — I would say "a hair of the dog that bit us," meaning, you know, a mouthful or two of ale to clear away the cobwebs left by the ale of the night before, but the thought of the hair of the dog we had with us made that figure of speech excessively unappealing — a mouthful or two of ale.

The pubkeeper had a word of advice for us, of course. Haven't you noticed that, whenever one is doing something, other people who are not doing it always have great heaping slathers of advice on how one should do it?

"Better stay close to the coast around here," he said. "It's safe enough just above land, but The Pirates of Bognor Regis skirt the beach, waiting for some nodcock to be blown just far enough out to sea for 'em to catch."

I thanked him, of course: one doesn't want to antagonize the chap preparing one's food and drink, after all, but shared a knowing wink with my fellow aeronauts.

~*~

Goggles in place, faithful dog whirring and clanking at the far end of the gondola, we fired up the engines and lifted off.

The elegant public buildings of Bognor Regis fell away below us.

"I say," Conkers shouted over the sound of the engines, "can you lower this a bit and go closer to the beach?"

"Why would I do that?" Everyone wants to tell one how to steer. It's enough to drive one mad.

"Girls," said Conkers. "Sea bathing."

Really, Conkers can be quite sensible, when he puts his mind to it.

I reduced the heat being channeled to the envelope (that's what we blimp-men call the balloon thing, you know) and pointed our nose to sea.

"Stop here! Stop here!" Minor and Conkers both screeched, as if volume would make a difference.

"It's all very well for you to say, 'Stop here,' but I can only control the rudder," I said, "not the ruddy wind!"

For, as I turned broadside to the beach, the wind caught the envelope and we slid sideways out and away from land.

"You muffleheaded chump!" Minor strode toward me. "Here — give me the rudder! Upon my word, my grandmother could steer better than you!"

"Bring your grandmother aboard, and I'll give her the rudder, but I jolly well won't give it to such a gormless duffer as you!"

As we struggled over control of the steering mechanism, I gradually became aware of Conkers' silly voice droning, "Chaps! I say, chaps! Here, you two! I say!"

When we paused to recruit our strength for another bout, Minor rounded on him.

"What is it, you bleating nitwit?"

Conkers only stared, seeming to be riveted by some sight behind us.

Minor and I turned.

A huge black airship with a white skull and crossbones emblazoned on the side was closing on us. It was near enough for us to see the evil grins of the men and women of the crew and the glint of their goggles.

Minor and I each let go of the rudder. In concert, we each said, "You take it! I'll add coal!"

We each lunged for the coal scuttle, bounced off each other, and fell to the gondola's floor. Dispossessed straw rose around us in a musty cloud.

"This is no time for you chaps to practice music hall routines," Conkers said. "I believe we're about to be boarded."

A grappling hook flew over the side of our basket and fastened firmly in the wickerwork. There was a violent jounce as it afixed itself and began pulling us toward the sinister vessel. A tell-tale clack and whizz spoke of Rex having tipped over and of his hapless struggle to right himself without the aid of a friendly toe.

Before one could say "Jack Robinson," which would have been a fairly useless thing to have said at such a time, the pirate ship was snugged against ours and a massive, muscular chap had joined us. He was flanked by two lieutenants, one male and one female, each brandishing muscles and flexing pistols. Er, the other way 'round, I think I mean.

Conkers stammered, "W-why? We aren't a cargo ship, you know. We aren't wealthy, or from wealthy families. Why capture us?"

The pirate chief's evil grin grew wider and, if possible, more evil.

"I can always use another ship for my fleet, even assuming you have no money with you, and you off on holiday. Then there's your food supplies. It may not be much, but it's something, eh? And don't underestimate the pleasure of watching you beg for your lives, and the diversion of wagering on how many times each of you will resurface before you drown."

Conkers spoke for us all: "Oh, I say!"

There was really nothing to add to that.

Apparently, Rex had managed to recover his feet, for he chose that moment to approach, stiff-legged, perhaps in response to some vestige of programming that instructed him to protect the person and property of his owner.

"Argh! Argh!" A low-pitched grating sound, possibly meant to be a growl, followed.

The pirate chief's grey eyes bulged and his jaw dropped. Had he never seen a clockwork dog before, or did he (and this was my preferred hypothesis) not realize that a clockwork dog is what he saw?

Both suppositions proved false, for he said,

"Rex! Rex, old boy!" The pirate chief sank to one knee, arms outstretched.

Rex hobbled over to him and allowed him to scoop him up, close to what one would previously have laid good odds was a heartless chest. Rex' flannel tongue swiped dry licks across the pirate's tear-dampened cheeks, leaving faint streaks of blue-black ink upon them.

The chief turned to his lieutenants. "This is Rex! My dear old playfellow! Often, I've told you how it crushed me when my uncle, whose ward I was, gave him away when I was in school."

The lieutenants looked as if they remembered very well, and that it had been jolly near once too often.

"Yes," one of them said. "Oxford, I believe. Senior year."

"It's why I became a pirate," said the vicious brute cuddling the clockwork canine. "I was trying — vainly, pitifully — to fill the void left by his loss. And here he is!"

It was all very touching, but I hope I won't be accused of lacking sentiment when I say that I was still somewhat concerned about our immediate future — mine and Minor's and Conkers', I mean.

"Go back aboard the ship," said the chief to his underlings. "Divide my share of all our loot amongst you. I mean to return to land with these lubbers, and lead a blameless life evermore."

He got no argument. In two shakes of a lamb's tail (though I don't see that a lamb shakes its tail at a greater velocity than any other frolicsome mammal), the pirates had left us, we were free of the grappling hook, and Rex' old master was plying the winds and easing us back to shore.

Once we landed, he put us out, took all our money,

food, and clothes (except for what we wore — one is, cutthroat or not, a gentleman), and informed us that he was taking the blimp to sell on the black market.

I pointed out a logical fallacy in that course of behavior: "I thought you meant to lead a blameless life evermore."

"True," he said, "but one must have a start."

A forceful argument, its persuasiveness bolstered by the pistol which he had retained from his life as a pirate.

"Will you leave us nothing?" Conkers can put on a convincing show of injured innocence. I've seen him stand before a mirror, practicing it, for hours before going to face a creditor. It usually buys him a few days' grace, and it didn't fail him, now.

A familiar pasteboard box sailed over the gondola's side, clattering as it landed in my arms.

"Not your old playfellow, surely!"

"Seeing him again brought me the closure I needed," said the former pirate. "Now, I must travel light. Farewell!"

From within the box, Rex answered, "Argh!"

~*~

We reported the theft, of course, and the police took to the skies in pursuit of the renegade. We never heard the result, but our flight insurance indemnified us against piracy, so at least we didn't have to reimburse the balloon chappie for the airship.

We finished our holiday in my own cozy rooms, pipes in our mouths, feet on the hob, dog snoring with a gentle birr.

"After all," said Minor, speaking for all of us, "there's no place like home."

"Very true," I said, eying the last of my bottled beer as it slid down Minor's gullet. "Why don't you go there?"

Dog Star

I'll begin with the dogs — *in medias Rex*, as it were. There were two of us — three, if you count Sparkle — four, if you count the puppy — but there were two of us on the scene.

Direct your attention, if you will, to Fiona. Cairn Terrier, twenty pounds of dark intensity, muscles and nerves of steel, wrapped in yards of gray shag. Observe her gleaming eyeteeth, her glittering eye. Do not attempt to extract that plastic action figurine from between her paws. She is not cuddling it, and she will not welcome your intervention. Fiona is my elder by three years, and I am five.

My name is Cyrano. I am, to an observable degree, Irish Setter. To her credit, Fiona, who is pedigreed and papered, purchased from a licensed breeder, has never made me feel my unmapped lineage.

The third dog in this adventure, the one we've never met, is a black Labrador retriever called Sparkle. Sparkle is the editor of "Sparkle's Bark," a newsletter to which I subscribe over the World Wide Woof. Every night, she sends out an issue filled with jokes, tips, and recipes.

Here's my favorite of Sparkle's recipes: Find a human who's eating a sandwich — road workers, construction workers, or kids are best — and sit where they can see you.

Don't make a sound or a move, just watch them eat. If desired, cock your head and prick up your ears if they look at you, or you may move your eyes or your head to follow the sandwich as it moves to and from the human's mouth. Before the sandwich is half gone, the human will either give you a piece of the sandwich or, ideally, remove one slice of bread and toss it to you.

I have personally tried this recipe many times, and I have never known it to fail.

So, when we found the Thing in the woods, it was only natural that I appealed to Sparkle for advice.

> *Dear Sparkle*, I barked.
>
> *My compatriot, Fiona, and I have run across a Hard Thing in the woods. It smells like Alive, but it doesn't move. It is very hard, and makes a metal noise when our tags knock against it. It sounds solid, not hollow. It is round, and about the size of a beach ball. It is smooth, like the side of a car, with three skinny and shiny legs. It is warm to the touch, even at night. Fiona bit one of the legs, and she said it tasted like Alive and like Bicycle at the same time. What should we do?*

Within the week, my question and an answer were in the "Ask Sparkle" section of "Sparkle's Bark":

> *Dear Cyrano,*
>
> *It sounds to me as if you have come across a large container of something, possibly el-evated on those legs in order to keep prowling animals out of it. This is very promising. First,*

get the Thing open; no doubt you will then know what to do. You don't say how long the legs are. If you can manage it, get its legs out from under it so it can't suddenly decide to run away! Once it's down, you can get your paws into opening it, assuming the fall doesn't crack it for you. Good luck!

Fiona and I immediately trotted into the moonlit woodland to where we had last seen the Thing earlier that evening.

It was still there. Stray moonbeams glinted off its gleaming black roundness and off the bright, thin legs. It made me hang my head to think that I had neglected to include information on its height in my message to Sparkle: it was taller than Fiona on her hind legs and slightly shorter than I am in that unnatural stance. I jumped at the Thing. It inched over the uneven ground. I jumped at it again. It rocked slightly, but it was well-balanced on its legs and the pivoting disk-shaped feet at their ends.

Fiona did not join my attack. She lay down flat, with her head on her paws, and regarded the Thing from under her brows, and a right unloving regard it was, too. When I saw that look, I stopped jumping, curled up comfortably in the underbrush, and waited. The thoughts of a Cairn Terrier are long, long thoughts, and will usually astound you when you realize what they are.

After the moon had lifted above the trees, Fiona stood and shook herself. Without looking at me, she trotted over to the Thing, saying, "When I give the word, jump at it again. Don't jump straight; come up from a crouch." With that, she went to the far side of the object and lay down with her side pressed against one of the legs.

I could see what she wanted, of course. I backed up and crouched. Shifted. Wiggled. Growled. *LEAPT!*

The Thing was heavy. When I, with Fiona as a fulcrum, knocked it off-balance, it teetered only a second or two, then went over. Fiona, with a Terrier's uncanny ability to avoid entrapment, slipped out of the way without the loss of so much as a single tail-hair.

I had feared that the soft earth, the moss and detritus of the shady floor, would cushion the Thing's fall. A happily placed outcropping of limestone just below the topsoil eliminated that fear: the Thing hit with a fang-jarring *clang*, rebounded from the force of its weight, and hit again. A seam opened right around the Thing's middle; if it had been upright, the seam would have been parallel to the ground. The top popped off and slid some yards across the clearing. With an acrid *whoof*, whatever had been inside ejected, scattering in a spray pattern from one part of the ruined Thing to the other. Smoke and flames roiled upwards, ruining our night vision and hampering our sense of smell.

Oops! Far from being a handy food container, this Thing appeared to be a machine, probably left here by a human, probably for a purpose he or she considered worthwhile. My only consolation was that it had no slightest scent of our personal people, so it probably had no business on our property in the first place. Perhaps we had done something Good and Noble unaware.

Fiona, closer to the ground than I, suffered less from the smoke than I did. She barked, growled, and circled the area between the two parts of the up-ended device.

"Something came out of it," she yapped at me.

"Something alive."

The fire flickered and died. I guarded one side of the sprayed remnants blindly, blinking my night vision back into play.

"It's moving," Fiona muttered between bared teeth.

Help me, said a voice inside my head.

"Did you hear that?" I asked Fiona. She growled in reply. Gingerly, I nosed through the debris.

"Careful — careful. . . ." I did not need Fiona's soft *woofs* to remind me, but I did appreciate them. She is a good dog to have at one's back, all in all.

I found the living thing in the ruins. It was about Fiona's size, wrapped in a cocoon of cloth.

Thank you, I heard. *You have saved me. Opening mechanism jammed. Starving in there. Starving now. Help. . . .*

"It wants to eat us," Fiona said.

No. . . .

"Wants a bite, anyway."

No. . . . Must be cooked. Must have plumage.

"It only eats chicken," I said.

Fiona wagged her stumpy tail in understanding. "I knew a poodle like that once. You only like it boiled?"

I do not know. All plumed flesh is the same. All prepared the same. Food is food.

Fiona coughed in disbelief. "I hate to think what Sparkle would have to say about that! Why, just in the past week, we've had—"

Please, came the unspoken voice. *Help me out of this suit. Carry . . . please.*

"Fiona — I think this is your field."

No dog alive is better at getting into what she was not

meant to than Fiona. It stood us in good stead now. She found the weak spot in the creature's wrapping before I could count to three, and soon worked the cocoon off and away.

The creature lay, a tiny hairless humanoid in silver skivvies, pathetically helpless at our feet. It lifted scrawny arms and waved them feebly. Each arm ended in hands, large in proportion to the rod-like arms, each with three fingers and an opposable thumb.

"How do I carry it?" I asked my companion. "I'm not putting it in my mouth. I don't know what it is, and Dog knows where it's been."

"Lie down next to it and let it climb on your back."

So that's what we did. I lay down on my side, and Fiona nudged it up against my fur and held it close to me until I rolled upright.

"Grrrrrrrrrrrrrrrrip!" Fiona ordered, and I felt a slight tug as the creature took double-handfuls of my fur.

I stood. "Now what?"

"We take it home."

"And do what with it?"

Take me to your leader. As it spoke this time, I was somehow given to know the creature was male, intelligent, in early middle age, and no more than moderately attractive to females of his species.

"Show him to the Lady?" I asked. "Or is Mister our leader?"

"Both of them. First thing in the morning."

The moon was sinking and the faint blush of false dawn stained the eastern sky as Fiona and I returned to our quarters. We shared a corner of the potting shed, insulated with hay bales and carpeted in discarded blankets. Our daily rations had long since been consumed, of course, but there were always a few stray crumbs in the folds of our bedding, carried there on our fur, to be searched out and consumed during late-night reminiscences or philosophical debates. There was, our Lady had assured us, at least a modicum of chicken involved in our rations' manufacture, and our guest seemed to bear this out. Having slid from my back, he sniffed until he turned up a few crumbs which he crunched in trembling desperation.

Better than nothing, he said, which is what we had always thought about it, too.

He uncovered and consumed a few more morsels, then said, *My name is Orton Scarro. I come from a galaxy far away, on the only habitable planet we ever found. I refused to give up the search, though. I became a laughingstock. My funding was pulled, I lost my job, my friends, my mate. . . .*

I whimpered.

"So you did what?" Fiona prompted. She hates it when I cry.

So I . . . well, I stole a ship that had been readied before the Council's vote to end all space exploration. It had been stored in an out-of-the-way facility while the debate dragged on and on, and had never been unloaded and dismantled. I took off, headed for nowhere in particular. The navigation program was random, purely exploratory, set to return when less than half the fuel was spent.

"What happened?" Fiona asked.

The creature named Orton Scarro lifted his empty hands. *I don't know. I mean, I know, but I don't know why. The programming identified a habitable planet — this planet — and landed safely and undetected, but the mechanism that opens the vehicle jammed. All the mechanisms jammed. The communicator wouldn't work, the nutrition tablet dispenser stopped dispensing, the life support system shut down to emergency bare minimum. It seems the liquid electrolyte holder developed a leak that circumvented all the fail-safes built into the system and shorted everything out. You saved my life. How did you know?*

"Canine instinct," said Fiona, while I said, "Dumb luck."

By this time, the sun was well up. I felt my ears lift at the sound of the patio door opening and the gritty step of our Lady's sandals on the cement. Next would come the rattle of Best Friend Protein Chunks With Real Chicken and Rice in our food bowls.

"Climb aboard," I told Orton. "Our leader has left the building."

Fiona and I trotted up to the patio, drawn by the scents of breakfast and our Lady's menthol filter-tip. She was wearing stay-at-home clothes — jeans and a shirt that read "My husband went to Alpha Centauri and all he brought me was this lousy t-shirt."

She greeted us as she usually did, with a jocular, "About time you dragged your lazy butts up here. Wore yourselves out barking all — What the hell is that?" That last bit, needless to say, was not usual.

I felt Orton's weight shift, and felt the clutch of one three-fingered hand release.

Our Lady squatted near me and peered at my passenger.

"It's an alien from outer space," she said. "*YES!*" She jacked herself up and slid the door open, yelling, "Andy!

Andy! You gotta see this!"

Mister came thumping out, his comfortingly hairy legs and chest bare, his Wile E. Coyote boxers bright and amusing in the early morning light. "This better be good, Kath."

"Look at this," our Lady said. "Look at what Cyrano brought up." She gestured at Orton, cigarette ash dusting the breeze.

He looked. "What is it?"

"Blink at him," our Lady told my rider.

"Damn!" said Mister.

My name is Orton Scarro, Orton "said." *Take me to your leader.*

"I think not," said our Lady, and sucked in a lungful of smoke. "If you knew any better, you wouldn't ask that. Proof positive you're from out of town."

"Right," Mister agreed. "They'd vivisect you till there wasn't any viv anymore. Then they'd ship what was left off to Area 51 and return all your mail marked 'no such person at this address.'"

"We have to help the little guy. I mean, what would Data do?"

If what you say is true, I am in great danger in my present form. I must disguise myself as a member of the indigenous population.

"Yeah." Mister knelt next to me. "Um. . . ."

I know Mister well enough to understand that what he meant was, "Something is happening, but I don't know exactly what, or whether or not I should be alarmed or even mention it."

The weight on my back grew greater, then disappeared as Orton slid to the patio with a fleshy double-flop. Flat feet.

Fiona barked.

I turned, and saw that Orton was twice the size he had been when we found him, and was growing as we watched. Mister leaned away and thumped back onto his rump. Our Lady flicked her cigarette butt into the dewy grass and helped Mister up; they clung together, watching Orton become a spindle-limbed, bald, pasty-skinned humanoid, still in silver skivvies, of the same general size as Mister.

Now I will blend in.

"Not quite yet, Flash Gordon," said our Lady. "Let's get you off the patio before you and Andy scandalize the neighborhood out here in your underwear. Andy, don't you have some clothes that would fit this new science fiction author who showed up at our doorstep with a proposal for a series of novels so detailed and authoritative they might have been written by an actual space traveler?"

Mister broke into a wide grin. "Katherine, you always were the best copywriter at Hovercraft Press."

She gave him a quick hug. "And you'll be the fastest-rising editor. They might even give you your own imprint."

"He'll need documents. . . ."

Show me what documents I need, and I can manufacture impeccable replicas for myself . . . if the ship's processor is still intact.

"How about fingers?" Our Lady wiggled her fingers and thumbs.

Orton counted them, then his own. *No. That I cannot do.*

Mister slid open the door and motioned the others in, saying, "Kath, call your brother at OSHA and see how long it would take a guy working at a non-compliant facility to lose two fingers. We need to brainstorm a background for our buddy here, anyway."

They took Orton inside, and we concentrated on our food, satisfied that we had done just as we ought.

Orton came out later, dressed in a pair of Mister's jeans and a t-shirt that said, "My other computer is a HAL 9000." He headed for the woods, so we just naturally went along. Orton owed us his life; the very least he could do, I thought, was take us walkies.

Your leaders are kindness itself, he said. *I believe I have landed in The Good Place.* Humming an unearthly tune, he led us back to his bipartite vehicle. The remains still lay scattered in a rough fan shape. Orton uprighted the bottom section. *Ah. The grid held.* He fiddled with something just under the open rim and lifted a large round wafer of silvery lattice and set it on the ground. *Yes. Good.* He touched something inside the black bowl on legs and a soft whispery shuffle barely reached my ears. *Good.* The whispering stopped. *Very good. Now let's see what else is still in order — or back in order.* He touched something else, and a high-pitched chatter erupted. Orton's eyes widened and his jaw dropped open. He covered his mouth with his long thin fingers and took a step back. He looked at us in desperate appeal, as if we understood what he heard, but the mind-talk seemed only to work in person.

Fiona shook her head. "No savvy. What did it say?"

They've found me! There must be a tracer beacon in these exploratory vehicles.

"Is that a problem?" I asked. "Well, true, you stole an expensive piece of equipment and wrecked it—"

Exactly! I am liable to the tune of eckrty-gifnul cradluks.

If dogs could whistle, I would have. I didn't know how much that was, but it sounded like more doggie treats than

I've ever seen in my life.

What am I to do? What am I to do?

"Pay them back when your science fiction blockbuster comes out," Fiona suggested.

But it is not out yet! I'll be executed before then! It's publish or perish, and I have not yet published!

There was only one thing to do.

"Don't panic," I said. "Clean up all this mess and cart everything back to the house. Get to work on that book, and I'll get help from an expert."

"Who?" Fiona asked.

"Sparkle — Who else?"

While Orton replaced the grid and piled it with debris Fiona fetched for him, I sat back and barked:

> *Dear Sparkle,*
> *Our new friend from outer space has an urgent problem. He comes from a planet where they only eat the same thing cooked the same way, so one can hardly blame him for stealing a vehicle and escaping. His problem is: they have found him, and are coming to execute him if he cannot repay the cost of what he stole. He has great expectations of a fortune (thanks to our humans) which will more than eliminate his debt, but he needs to begin payment immediately. Any suggestions?*

When I had finished, I felt much better. I helped Orton and Fiona clean up, and we soon had capped the sphere. Orton lifted it and staggered with it out of the woods and across the lawn onto the patio, where he set it down with a *clash.*

"Now," I said, "get in there and start writing!"

He patted each of us absently and went in.

I hardly expected a reply to so knotty a problem in less than a week, possibly not ever. Sparkle might easily have thought me a crack-pot or a joker, but the tone of my bark must have been conveyed to her along with the content of my message, for she answered that very evening.

> *Dear Cyrano,*
>
> *When I heard of your friend's problem, I considered it at first beyond my scope. Happily, though, your fellow subscribers have (I believe) come to the rescue, as they have so many times before. Several others along the line of transmission appended the following information, which I knew but did not recall until they brought it to my attention: The humans have a service almost identical to mine. It's called "World Wide Recipes — the best darned recipezine in the whole darned universe." It is run by a human known as "The Chef," whose motto is "Be Nice — Nice Is Good." Surely such a human could — and would — help. Tell your friend to get on that human version of the World Wide Woof, go to www.worldwiderecipes.com, and subscribe.*

"What do you think?" I asked Fiona.

"Wouldn't hurt to try. — Orton! Orton!" Fiona's barks are short and sharp and piercing, reaching the threshold of pain at their terminations. The power of them lifts her clear of the ground with every yowp. Orton opened a window in the second floor and leaned out.

Fiona explained Sparkle's suggestion. Orton leapt at the possibility of rescue. Half an hour after Fiona had communicated Sparkle's message, Orton leaned out of his window again.

I signed up, and I sent a cry for help to The Chef. Now I can only wait. Wait and hope.

"And write!" Fiona shouted. Fiona coaches cheerleading for dogfights.

The next day was very tense, enlivened only by Orton's delight in discovering new foods and sharing them with his first friends on the planet — Fiona and myself.

That evening, as we awaited the arrival of "Sparkle's Bark," we heard an excited babble from inside the house. The patio door slid open, and Orton clopped out in green-and-white Hawaiian print shirt and shorts and a pair of Andy's cast-off Earth Shoe sandals. He waved a piece of paper, laughing triumphantly and headed straight for his ship — for the communications device within it, rather.

He emailed me back! he told us as he removed the ship's top half, then the grid which fit like a second, flat, lid. *Listen:*

> *Dear Orton:*
> *Sorry I took so long getting back to you. At first I thought it was a joke, or that you were some kind of crack-pot! Then the funniest thing happened. I read your message aloud to my family, and our black lab puppy jumped up and started wagging her tail. Just for laughs, I asked her if she*

thought you were for real, and she jumped up and around — what I call "franticulating." I figure, if you can't trust a dog, who can you trust? So I emailed a few of my regular subscribers and correspondents and they all suggested the same thing: I'm going to make you the exclusive interstellar distributor of the World Wide Recipes ezine. Every weekday, your people will have access, through you, to two of my personal favorite recipes; A Word From The Chef; two food funnies; a kitchen tip; the "Ask the Chef" feature; the Pen Pal Forum, where our readers submit their own recipes on a theme they choose; the Bulletin Board, where readers request recipes and advice or post food-related announcements; and a Last Morsel, which defies description, but is like the perfect dessert. The interstellar yearly subscription rate to World Wide Recipes is usually $25 per sentient being (less than fifty US cents per week), but I am willing to allow you — and you only — to distribute it to your people at absolutely no charge, provided they will write off the equipment you stole and spare your life. Ask any of my adoring readers — it's a bargain at the price!

Thanks for subscribing.
The Chef

Orton hooted and waved the paper aloft. *Saved! I am saved!*

I thought he was being a little previous, but it seems he

knew his people well. He stuck his head into the base of his spacecraft and spoke at length, referring to his paper occasionally. We could hear nothing, but the way his four-toed feet all but danced on the patio's cement and the way his saggy bottom swayed and jiggled made it obvious the negotiations were going well.

Thus it was that Orton's life was saved, an entire planet was delivered from culinary ennui, and science fiction gained a new super-star. Orton moved into the house next door and took down the fence between the yards, so Fiona and I have more room to "franticulate." Mister bored some holes in the bottom of Orton's three-legged space module to increase the draft; with its grids back in place, it makes a dandy patio grill. Many a cook-out we've all enjoyed together (Orton still has a weakness for grilled chicken), and Orton always manages to slip Fiona and me dishes of tasty skin and gristle — Now that's good eating!

Sure Thing

I used to say I never met a Greenhorn I didn't like, but Middle-C-F-Sharp-A was about to become the first exception. Maybe I shouldn't have took him to the track with me, but there was always a flock of them there, having a good time, so I took him.

He knew I was ticked when I whistled his real name instead of calling him by the official Earth American one Immigration assigned him: Peter Bluefeather.

Pete was about my height, his green skin dark from working next to me on the farm. Two tufts of yellow feathers stuck up like horns from the sides of his head; the one blue one on the left gave him his Earth American surname.

Orange beak, red flag, like we say, and Pete's was orange now. He was a sucker for a racetrack tout; bet a hot tip every race and lost every time. He'd just paid another ten bucks for another one.

I whistled the Greenhorn phrase for *Don't start.*

He clacked his bill twice then held it open a couple of seconds, working his round pink tongue.

Between the Earth American he'd learned and the Greenhorn whistles he'd taught me, we did okay on the farm. Harder for him than it was for me, though, because I always been a good whistler, and he had to make lip sounds without any lips.

"Man go," he said.

"What man goes where?"

"*Man*-go. *Man*go." He shook his racing form at me and handed it over.

There was a circle around a horse in this race — the last race — named Mango, at 11-1.

"Oo, too," Pete said.

So far, I had picked my own horses and broke even, plus enough to buy us hot dogs and beers. Maybe that second beer wasn't a good idea for Pete, because now he wanted to seal our friendship by sharing his hot tip with me.

"How about *you* bet on *my* horse?"

I could tell by the way he cocked his head, he'd sulk for days if I didn't give in.

I whistled agreement and we put our money on Mango.

When they played the Call to the Post, Pete twittered laughter along with the other Greenhorns; seems that phrase was a smutty joke in one of their languages.

And the horses raced.

The one I would have bet on came in first. Mango is probably still running, if he ain't died of old age.

You never seen a sorrier-looking Greenhorn than Pete, outside of moulting season.

When we was about halfway home, I heard him mutter something the first guy he worked for taught him:

"Pete's a dirty bird."

It like to broke my heart.

"Pete ain't no kinda bird."

I whistled his real name — Middle-C-F-Sharp-A, then I

whistled *The Isle of Capri*, which I learned early on is the same tune as a Greenhorn formal statement of friendship.

We whistled it in harmony the rest of the way home.

Pile-up

The jingle played again on the radio, the third time I'd heard it this morning, to and from shopping at the Lady Plus outlet:

The fatter you are, the better you fly!
Successful dieters need not apply.

For some reason, I actually listened to the man in the ad this time, instead of dismissing the announcement as a particularly insensitive commercial for a diet club.

Are you overweight? Have you tried everything and been unsuccessful? Sky-High Support is now taking applications for its new training program. Some risk is involved, so applicants without dependents are preferred.

He gave the time and location — now and nearby.

I was the perfect applicant: In my mid-twenties, I'd started picking up weight. I'd cut back on calories, stepped up exercise, and still gained weight. When I reached a certain age and a certain number of pounds over my optimal size, my husband filed for divorce. We had no children. My parents were financially solid. So, no dependents. And risk sounded good this morning.

When I walked into the lobby of the hotel hosting the application fair I saw I wasn't the only one attracted by the offer. Unwanted fat men and women piled up about the conference room door like teens at a rock concert, but with fewer of us per square inch.

The door opened and we filed in. A man who could have been a poster boy for the organization handed us each a clipboard equipped with a stack of papers and a tethered pen.

"Take a seat and fill these out. Take a seat and fill these out." His voice never lost its animation, no matter how often he said it. His eyes sparkled as brightly as the buckle on his triple-X belt.

They ran out of applicants before they ran out of chairs. Not all unwanted fat men and women are willing to admit to either state.

I looked over the papers while I waited for the doors to close and for somebody to tell me what this was all about. The papers gave nothing away. They were health histories, HIPA forms, employment histories, interest evaluations, and personality tests. Nothing about the organization.

After about fifteen minutes, the man at the door closed it and said, "Anybody finished filling out the papers?" Some hands went up. "Anybody started?" A few more hands. "Okay, if you've started or finished, please move to the next room."

When they were gone and the door had shut behind them, he said, "Those are the first wash-outs. We're not looking for the kind of people who would fill out papers without knowing what the papers were for. As for the rest of you, welcome to the first cut for the Support Program. Here's what we do: We train you to go into dangerous situations and retrieve people. Might be hostage situations, might be a fall in hard-to-reach terrain, might be the debris of a wreck or a collapsed building."

More than one voice couldn't help saying, "*Fat people?*"

"Fat people." He patted his chest. "I've logged over a thousand hours in field rescue. The Sky-High Support Program tests you to make sure you can't lose weight under any normal circumstances, does blood work to make sure you're healthy; then, if you get through those cuts, we train you for rescues."

We all cut looks at each other. I couldn't picture myself climbing up and down mountains or working my way through train wrecks. And it seemed like, if somebody was trapped under ten tons of rubble, the last thing they'd want is another two hundred or so on top of that. Still, the opportunity was too good to pass up. The worst that could happen would be that we'd fail the second cut by losing weight — not a failure any of us would regret.

~*~

That happened to most of us, during the months of healthy diet and strength training. Most of the rest quit when the diet got *too* healthy and the training got *too* rigorous. Finally, out of the original 150, ten of us were left.

The program's doctor drew blood and sent us home.

I hadn't lost an ounce. If anything, I'd gained a pound or two, although my weight might vary by as much as five pounds from one day to another, so it was hard to tell. I felt good, though. The wholesome food and exercise invigorated me. I could walk without puffing and could get in and out of the car without three practice *oofs*. Whatever happened, going through the program had been worth it.

The call came the next day. My blood work was good. I was part of Sky-High Support! The investiture was scheduled for the following Monday.

~*~

"Congratulations, ladies and gentlemen!"

The investiture took place in the gym where we'd suffered through so much of our physical training. We had done no climbing practice, which seemed odd, but I reasoned that they were saving that for the finalists. No sense training the people who weren't going to make the final cut, though all of the ten who finished the program were here.

"Repeat after me."

I solemnly swear to answer the call to rescue those in peril, to reserve my power for the exercise of my duty, never to abuse my abilities, and always to behave in a way that reflects honor on Sky-High Support.

"Welcome to the most elite volunteer rescue brigade in the world. Your real training is about to begin."

I had a feeling we were about to get some more drop-outs. I was sweating already.

Freddy, the man who'd given us the clipboards and sworn us in smoothed the front of his polo shirt and said, "How many of you are sick of people telling you how light on your feet you are?"

All our hands came up.

"Well, guess what? They're right."

A couple of our trainers, almost as hefty as Freddy, pulled back the accordion wall that had always blocked the far end of the gym.

Ah! A climbing wall, with a dummy dangling by ropes from the top.

Freddy pointed at it. "There's your rescue target. Here's the protocol: First, let him know he's been spotted. Second, tell him you're coming to help him. Third, go get him. One, two, three, just that simple. Okay. Somebody called us out to find a lost hiker. I'm up on the roster, so I go out. I spot him."

Freddy cupped his hands and shouted, "You're going to be all right. Hang on. I'm coming up for you." And he raised his arms above his head and lifted off the ground and, as God is my witness, he flew up to the dummy. He took some kind of harness from his belt and fastened it around the "rescue target", turned in the air to slip his arms through a pair of straps, lifted far enough to disengage the ropes holding the dummy in place, and gently descended to the floor.

"And that, boys and girls, is how it's done."

He explained that, just as it had been discovered there was a gene for a tendency to put on weight and keep it on, there was another component to that gene. What we had and couldn't shed wasn't fat, it was another substance that was fat-like but had anti-gravitational properties, which could be activated by mental control and manipulated by physical control.

My fellow inductees and I swapped stunned glances. I saw disbelief dawning into delighted realization as dreams and urges I would bet we'd all had suddenly made sense.

So that's my story. And I've finished it just in time: Here comes your Medi-Copter. Wave down at the reporters again, and try not to be mad at them. A ten-car pile-up is news, and you're the only one who couldn't at least crawl away. Man trapped in car, flames closing in, daring aerial rescue. . . . You'll be all over the news for a couple of days. Me? No, not me. I'm just doing my job. Nothing news-worthy about that.

Western Star

Leland pinned the tin star on his vest and buckled his gun belt. He fitted the immersion mask over his face and said, "Wild West Gunfight on."

The smell of hot dust and drying horse droppings filled the mask. He tasted whiskey and unfiltered tobacco, with the foul undertone of medium-rare steak. He should have specified he was vegetarian, but he hadn't expected the reality to go as far as this.

He shifted his weight from foot to foot and felt himself stride, spurs jingling, down the street he saw passing to either side. The sun was high and hot.

A horse neighed farther along the street. A man in black stepped from behind the horse, shaking his gloved hands to limber them.

"That's far enough, Sheriff," the man said.

"This is my town . . . er . . . Blackie," Leland said, hoping the session wasn't being recorded for quality control. What a lame name for the bad guy! But nobody had told him he'd have to make up names — he'd put that in his evaluation, for sure: Instruct users what, if any, creativity obligations they will encounter, and/or supply appropriate choices for them to use. "In my town, I say what's far enough."

Pretty good line. He wouldn't be embarrassed if they caught that one on tape.

"Slap leather," Blackie said.

Leland remembered that "slap leather" was on the list of gunfight challenges.

"Make your move," he replied.

In slow motion, Blackie's hand went to his hip. In slow motion, Blackie drew his gun.

Leland watched, rooted and stock-still, as the gun's barrel rose and moved, more and more slowly, glacially lining up with his heart. He was supposed to draw and fire, his opponent programmed to lose.

Blackie's gun stuck in mid-aim. His arm trembled with the strain of turning it on Leland. His mouth twisted in a snarl. His face reddened with effort.

One word slid through his teeth, oiled by fury. *"Draw!"*

Everything went black-and-white, then red, then black-and-white, while a buzzer sounded *Aaah! Aaah! Aaah!*

An ever-so-slightly mechanical male voice announced, "Program terminated due to disuse. Please reset and re-initiate program. If you have encountered a problem with your equipment or experience, please—"

Leland removed the helmet with shaking hands. He pricked his finger as he undid the sheriff's badge and put it, with the mask, on the testing room table.

He never wanted to run into that Blackie character again. He had a feeling that, next time, Blackie wouldn't bother with meeting him face-to-face. Next time, he'd be playing poker or riding through the dusk and he'd get a bullet in the back. No, somebody else could test the Wild West module. Unlike the VR engineers, Leland knew when to quit.

Aardvark with an Arrow

Everybody had aardvarks that year, remember?

One cute aardvark hologram on the etherwaves had sparked a dozen more, then the merchandizing kicked in, then the 'waves were littered with nodes celebrating the wonderfullness of all things aardvark.

ReeMarie had that hit single, "Your Aardvark Eats The Ants In My Heart" so, naturally, ReeMarie had to have one. The wonder is she didn't get a dozen. No, the wonder is the poor animal survived.

I'm responsible for that. Celebrity aardvark wrangler is not what my parents had intended for their son, but the job market popped up along with the craze. Ant breeder was another big job boom, but entomology was never my strong suit. I'd rather herd a 150-pound mammal than deliver 25-pound boxes of ants and termites to the back entrances of pet shops and McMansions.

I just happened to be window-shopping at the pet store when ReeMarie popped in on a whim. The aardvark on display was still a cuddly baby, mostly hairless, all wrinkly, with those big rabbit ears and no claws to speak of yet, so its little pink paws looked like stubby fingers.

"I thought they had *hair*," ReeMarie said, pulling her

head back from the display tank and scrunching up that handsome nose of hers.

"They do, when they're grown," I said. "Hair, and claws that can rip through concrete. They weigh up to 150 pounds, full grown."

I hoped all that would discourage her, but she said, "You seem to know all about 'em. You work here?"

"No. I work . . . elsewhere." I worked at a fast food joint, but I didn't need to tell her that. "I just always liked aardvarks."

"Before my song?"

"Yes." Then, being no fool, I added, "More, *after* your song, though."

"I don't know a thing about them." She said this as if it would surprise me, so I acted surprised. She stared at the little guy in the tank for a while, then said, "I *ought* to have one."

"You could get a stuffed one." Then I heard what that might imply and said, "A plush one, I mean, not a *real* stuffed *real* one, obviously. Maybe one to match each outfit you wear."

"That's fake," she said, curling that cute upper lip. "There is nothing whatsoever fake about me." She rolled her shoulders, making the rolly bits below her shoulders roll, too. "You want a job? Taking care of it? The aardvark? For me? I was going to look for somebody in the Yellow Pages, but I like it that we've met face-to-face. Besides, this makes a better story for the reporters."

She named a monthly salary twice my current yearly take, and I pretended to consider it for a couple of seconds, then agreed.

The pet shop carried a full range of aardvark supplies, so she arranged for a water bowl, a feeding station, a padded sleeping den and a week's worth of ant/termite mix to be delivered to her local home. She also bought an off-the-rack harness and leash, though she planned to have him measured weekly and new hand-tooled and bejeweled ones made as he grew. I put the harness and leash on him, but tucked him under my leather jacket and carried him in my arms.

She named him Valentine. Taking my plush suggestion, she had outfits made for him to complement hers: leg warmers, collars, hats, T-shirts, necklaces, belts. He tolerated it all. Aardvarks are actually good-natured, if they're raised by hand from a young age.

But you know that. And you know how I became a minor celebrity myself, as ReeMarie's Valentine's wrangler. And you know how I nudged ReeMarie into becoming a champion of animal rights, and about the books I wrote on aardvark care and training, and the kids' book, VALENTINE'S BIG ADVENTURE, which ReeMarie illustrated — who knew she could draw so beautifully? — with all proceeds going to the Aardvark Rescue League.

Then the fad passed. Aardvarks went out of favor, and it didn't take more than a year. As I told ReeMarie, they get big — BIG — and they live for over twenty years. Most of the people who bought real ones during the craze lost interest in the animals when the fashion moved on to pangolins.

"I can't be out of date," she told me, when she handed me my pink slip. "Plus, I'm established now. I don't need a gimmick. It just makes me look like I'm grabbing for attention, and I don't need to do that."

I couldn't just walk away, though. "What about Valentine?"

"He's yours." She handed me an envelope. "I thought you might ask. Just in case you did, I had these drawn up. I transferred ownership of Valentine to you. And ownership of that little place I bought in Indiana for him to play in."

That little place was five acres of woodland with a house and barnyard. It was amazingly generous.

"Thank you. I don't know what to say. Thank you."

She looked away. "You're a good guy. I'm gonna miss you. I'd keep you on, but I don't need the aardvark."

By "aardvark", she meant "expense". Fame is almost as fleeting for singers as it is for exotic pets. ReeMarie's revenues were sinking and her retinue needed shrinking. If she wanted to hop out of the category of Flavor-of-the-Month and try for Industry Icon, she needed to simplify her profile, cut back on costs, trade extravagance for gravitas.

She smiled. "I'm gonna miss Valentine, too. Just when I was getting into him." She had been spending more time with us, taking refuge with his quiet snuffling, quizzing me about his habits and preferences and peculiarities.

She gave a laugh with no amusement in it. "The things we do for success, huh? Sometimes I wonder if it's worth it."

A whole waterfall of understanding cascaded through my brain and washed away all my cluelessness.

"Listen, ReeMarie," I said. "You've taken care of me these months. Paid me well, *and* paid my way. I've got money in the bank." I flapped the envelope with the deeds in it. "And now this. If the time ever comes. . . . If the time ever comes that you want off the merry-go-round, there's a man and his aardvark waiting for you in Indiana."

She smiled straight at me, then, those gorgeous eyes shining. "I'll keep that in mind," she said. "I most certainly will."

And she did.

Reading From the Book of First Bambi

1. In the land of Corydon, there dwelt a man who kept a garden.
2. He had a dog who rolled and dug in the freshly turned earth, and the man cursed him roundly.
3. He had tomato plants and kale and cabbage and asparagus, and insects did eat them and lay eggs between their leaves, and he cursed the insects.
4. He had strawberries and beans, and rabbits did eat the plants, lo, even down to the soil line, and the man cursed the rabbits.
5. He had cucumbers and squash, and turtles did eat them, and he cursed the turtles.
6. He had blueberries, and deer did come up, yea, even within sight of the dog, and ate the blossoms off, and the man cursed the deer.
7. He also cursed the dog again, for good measure.
8. Now, the man had a pair of pruning shears, which he used to trim off any dead or unproductive plant growth, or any bit he termed "a sucker," which drew energy from the part of the plant he wanted to be strong.

9. One day, he put the shears down and went inside for tea and got a phone call during which he and his friend would have solved all the problems of the world, if only the people in power had taken their advice,
10. Then he remembered he needed to paint the porch,
11. Then he decided to strip and re-wax the kitchen floor,
12. Then he turned on some music and took a nap.
13. When he went back to work, he had forgotten where he put the shears and he never found them again.
14. And centuries passed, and men and the children of men walked no more upon the earth.
15. Nor their little dogs, either.
16. Ungulants and lagomorphs developed opposable thumbs and worked side-by-side in the garden.
17. And they cursed the insects and the turtles.
18. And the God of Irony looked down, and saw that it was good.

AMEN

Slob v Snob

Jonathan had always detested dystopian, post-apocalyptic literature. It irritated him beyond telling to now be living in such a world. Irony was a bitch.

His one point of brightness was that he had been provident enough to lay in a goodly supply of excellent boots. They were heavy but almost silent, with soles thick enough protect his feet from the rubble, and to hold him above the muck.

A sucking, rattling rasp warned him in time to stop. The yellow gob, with iridescent white foam quivering atop it, landed in front of him instead of on his trousers.

Two badly shaven men shambled out of the alley to his right, grinning, their teeth still straight and whole from pre-apocalyptic dentistry, but filthy from post-apocalyptic personal lack of hygiene.

They began a rhetorical call-and-response ritual, the overture to the main feature: violence.

"Whadda we got here?"

"Wull, it looks like one o' them fancy Bookers."

"Naw, he ain't no Booker." A grimy hand, one grimy finger extended, poked him in the chest. "You a Booker? Eh? You *read?*"

"I bet he reads them *hard* books."

"That right?"

Irony being a bitch with a sense of humor, the Hocker who had asked about hard books was struck in the head by one, and stumbled into the street. The face of the Hocker who had poked Jonathan now slackened into panicked pleading.

"Sorry," Jonathan said. "The Bookers are expanding their territory. Bookers claim Norrel Avenue. Tell your friends, if you have any."

The Hocker dove back into the alley, giving his associate up for lost. Jonathan watched avidly as bespectacled men and women converged on the fallen Hocker, pelting him with mass market paperbacks and the occasional slim volume of verse.

When they retreated to their new front-line headquarters, Jonathan knelt by the bleeding man. The Hocker's eyelids fluttered. Breath wheezed through his open mouth, his nose swollen and his nostrils stuffed with pages.

It was better when they were alive. Fresh food was so much better for you.

Jonathan had always hated zombie stories, too. Oh, irony!

The One and Only

I never thought I'd ever get to actually see Rani Barlow in person. Never thought I'd get to talk to her on Skype or text with her or email her, or she'd read my blog every day. Never thought we'd be best friends. But it happened.

Of course, you know how they say, "I wouldn't talk to you if you were the last man on earth"? Pretty much it.

The scientists kept telling us to stay calm and wash our hands frequently and avoid crowds and don't travel, but whatever it was that everybody was calling The Plague just kept spreading.

Every day, we expected them to come up with a vaccine or a cure or something, but they never did. This time, they never did.

At first, I hardly noticed the difference. I spend most of my time in my room, anyway, telecommuting to my job, playing online games, video chatting — you know, an active professional and personal life.

I didn't know the company folded until the direct deposits stopped. The banks closed not long after that. Players dropped out of the multi-player games until it was just me against the program, and then the program stopped running. People stopped answering when I paged them.

It was weird, going to my social networks and seeing the activity streams just sit there, with no updates ticking by.

I switched from looking at people I knew to global view, and was kind of relieved to see that other people were still around.

Not, you know, *around* around, but alive. The ones who could speak English and I were happy to connect, but every day we lost more of our new network than we added.

Then there was just me.

Maybe they weren't dead. Maybe their part of the power grid just went down and they didn't know what to do about it. That happened to me, after a while.

So I took whatever electronics and batteries I could fit in my backpack and picked a car and started driving, looking for signs of life.

Food wasn't a problem. When I got hungry or thirsty, I raided a grocery store. I broke into diners and made coffee every morning. I kind of had to go practically vegetarian, because meat and dairy don't last long without refrigeration, although I did have canned meat, and of course that orange cheesy stuff that comes in the big blocks — that lasts forever.

I checked the net every day, and I updated my blog every day. My visitor count was, like, zero, but I kept on, hoping somebody would find me.

And she did. She left the first comment my blog had had for months. I was like, *OMG! Rani Barlow? Are you punkin' me? Really? Really? Because I am such a fanboy!*

She was really nice! She gave me her contact info, and I called and we Skyped. I was actually, really, literally talking face-to-face with Rani frickin' Barlow!

When she gave me her address and asked me to come

out there, I couldn't believe it. She said she'd rather come meet me halfway so we could see each other sooner (!!), but she was taking care of her mom and some other people (I told you she was nice!) and she couldn't leave them.

So I headed out there, gassing up the car when I found a pump that worked, switching to another car that still had gas when I didn't have any luck with gassing up what I was driving.

Every day, I updated my blog about my adventures, just for Rani. Every day, we talked when she wasn't taking care of her sick people. Every day, she looked sadder and more stressed out, and cried when we talked because her mom or somebody else had died.

I was within a day's drive when she stopped answering my calls. Instead of breaking into a motel room for the night, I decided to push on and see my movie star friend as soon as possible.

She told me the last time we talked to just walk into the house, that the door was unlocked, so I did. The smell really took me back in time. It had been so long since I'd smelled fresh death, I got kind of nostalgic, if that makes any sense. It was almost like having people around, you know?

I went looking for the room Rani had Skyped me from, and I found it. And I found her.

I hadn't missed her by much. She was stretched out on a couch, and she almost looked like she was asleep, except that her beautiful violet eyes were open. And, honestly, they weren't very beautiful anymore.

So I was alone again. But at least I got to see Rani Barlow in person, sort of.

Scratch that off my Bucket List.

Til Death Us Do Part

Adhara rubbed her forehead as she stepped out of the arrival chamber.

The tech put a hand to Adhara's elbow and steered her to a chair, folding the disposable pad around her shivering nudity.

"Everything looks fine," he said, eyes on the readings, not on her body.

"What happens if it doesn't?"

He smiled. "We don't even think about that."

Adhara had been thinking about it, though — more, every time she transported. What if something interfered with the signal between Point A and Point B? What if the Adhara who was materialized at Point B was "significantly different" from the one at Point A? "Outside standard tolerances, as laid out by Interstellar Legislation"?

Had it happened? Had nascent Adharas been dis-materialized, and the signal resent?

And how did they know — How *could* they know — about all the possible differences?

A chime signaled the readiness of her personal effects: the one-day wardrobe she had ordered, the single-use cosmetics, the wedding ring surrogate.

Ten minutes after leaving Indiana, Adhara stepped into the thin London sunshine.

A line of robbies — Britain's name for what Americans called robocops — held back the vocal protestors who still greeted everybody who left the transport station with shouts of "Golem!" and, most inexplicably, "Get! a! soul! Get! a! soul!"

The robbies kept the crowd at bay while Adhara waved down a taxi and gave the driver the address of Grayson London.

"Loonies," the taxi-man said. "Get a soul? What's that meant to say, then? Like it sucks out your soul, ridin' in a taxi?"

"No." Adhara shifted and took in the interior of the vehicle, shabby and innocuous. "They weren't talking about the taxi."

"I know that, don't I? But I mean, you get in the taxi, I drive you to 4213 Baysington Road, you get out." He cut the air three times, three places: "You. You. You. Right?"

"Yes, of course."

"What's the difference, then, eh? What's the difference between a taxi and a transport, eh? Suckin' your soul! That's rubbish. What a load o' rubbish, eh? Innit?"

"Rubbish," she echoed, thinking about the transport home, after this day's meeting was over.

~*~

The ancient organ wheezed, up in the choir loft. Adhara read the prayer from the service app on her mini-tablet. Taavi had slept in, as usual, and had tried to persuade her to stay in bed with him for a morning of love and news, coffee and toast.

She couldn't remember the last time she'd been to mass,

but she had felt compelled, this morning. She had stepped out of the transport station at the end of her business trip hungry for Sunday.

It was the Feast of the Ascension, and Father Gephart spent his nine minute homily assuring them of life after death. He passed around the Eucharist without hesitation. No accusations of soullessness here. The church had declared the spirit a gift of Grace, firmly attached to the Person by the . . . surely the encyclical hadn't called it the epoxy of Christ Jesus. Surely that had been a late-night comic.

Or was it a shadow memory, sparked by a neuron firing where no neuron had been in the physical brain she'd had before this trip had dissolved it, reformed it, dissolved it and reformed it again? The one she'd been born with, before all the commutes by transport?

She took the wafer on her tongue as if it really was the Bread of Life, tears burning her eyes as they hadn't since her first communion, long before human transport was common.

A surreptitious scan of the congregation as she shuffled back to her pew showed her more than a few strained faces. More than one head bowed over hands clasped tightly on jittering knees. More than one fist laid over more than one heart jerked in a rhythm easily deciphered as, "By my fault, by my fault, by my most grievous fault."

Again, in the benediction, the Father instructed them that the Lord held their souls in his sight and in his hands at all times. The news had been full of a new rash of suicides that morning; no doubt, he wanted no copycat rash in *his* parish.

~*~

"What was she like?" Adhara paused the hologram she wasn't

really watching, anyway.

Taavi, his eyes fixed on the virtual page of his newsprint, shrugged irritably.

That means he hears me but he doesn't want to answer. How strange that I know that.

"What was she like?" She dismissed the program and called up a picture of Adhara Brisbane before her last trip. She divided the holoscreen and snapped a picture of herself, putting it and the older picture side-by-side. "Compare," she said.

The program claimed they were identical, but that meant nothing. There was a certain margin of error, and it was in the corporate/government interest to claim identicality.

"Do you miss her?"

Taavi flicked away his newsprint and turned toward her with red cheeks and narrowed eyes.

"There is no 'her' to miss. There is only you. You."

What did she see in him? She wished the Adhara who had married him were around, so she could ask her. *He's handsome, in an over-ripe sort of way, and he has a steady job, but he's shallow and prickly and not really terribly bright.* If she could go back in time, she would warn herself against him.

Of course, if she could go back in time, she could warn herself against transporting. Except that then she wouldn't have anything to warn herself against, so she wouldn't. Except that she wouldn't have listened to herself. It isn't as if nobody had sounded any warnings about the possible effects. The talking heads had chewed the subject to rags — were still chewing it, in fact. The tolerances for data transfer variance were so fine as to be considered zero, but a lot of little almost-zeroes could still add up to something.

The protestors were protesting the wrong thing. There might or might not be a God. God might or might not preserve the soul intact from one materialized Adhara to the next. But a body dissolved and reformed, and it didn't take a lot to screw with that.

Taavi jerked and snapped off his newsprint, but not before Adhara had seen why: another story of another rebooting gone wrong.

Illegal in most countries, rich people could still find clinics somewhere that would take an old datapack, dis-materialize an aging client and re-materialize him or her at a younger age with or without preserving the intervening mental changes. There were even some who claimed they could tweak the data and change your gender, health profile, boob size or anything else you ordered.

More and more people were trying it, which meant more and more stories giving people who couldn't afford rebooting reason to congratulate themselves. This latest, which Adhara had already heard, was about an aging rock star who now couldn't remember how to play an instrument or read music. He looked like thirty, but all he wanted to do was putter in his garden and sit in the sun.

Everyone considered it a tragedy except the star, who was more than happy to retire on the money some other self had made.

"Would you love me if I came back different?"

Taavi switched off the light and reclined his half of the bed, his back to her. "We are not having this conversation."

~*~

"As an attorney," Jacinta said, "I'm probably violating professional ethics by turning down money." She paused to give Adhara time to join her in a tension-breaking chuckle, which didn't happen. Giving up on the humor, she said, "Okay, on the clock." She pressed a mark on her desk. "Billable time has begun. Adhara Brisbane. State your business."

"I want a divorce."

"State name of spouse."

"Taavi Brisbane."

"No fault?"

"He's unfaithful."

"Do you know who he's being unfaithful with?"

"With me. He's being unfaithful with me."

"Allow me to restate: You wish to divorce your husband because he loves you."

"It isn't me! He's faithful to the me he married, but that isn't me anymore."

"You realize that anyone in any marriage since the beginning of marriages could say the same thing, right?"

"I'm not being philosophical."

Jacinta sighed. "I know. I also know that judges don't just grant 'transport differences' divorces. If you file with those grounds, you're guaranteeing yourself six months of couples counseling and three months of personal therapy for you, yourself. That's even if Taavi doesn't contest the filing."

"Do you ever transport?"

The lawyer nodded. "Several times a day. It's the quickest way to get to court. Pop in on the other side of the security checkpoint in the Attorney Chamber, dress in the clothes I keep in my locker there, and I'm good to go."

"Don't you ever feel. . . ."

"Different? No, I don't. I know who I am, and it would

take more than some micro-slippage to change that. The law doesn't recognize it: the 'Beam Me Up Scotty' defense has never been allowed. Not once. Transporting isn't a mitigating circumstance." She held up both hands, each one representing an aspect of the defense. "If you did it before transporting, you're still guilty after transporting. If you did it after transporting, you can't blame data slippage for diminished responsibility."

She touched the mark on her desk again. "Off the record, I don't understand this disorder."

"You mean the protestors?"

"No, the Disorder. Transport Syndrome Disorder. Personal advice: get help."

She re-engaged the recording. "As your attorney, I advise you to file no-fault."

~*~

Dr. Sargo tapped his electronic tablet with the stylus. "And who diagnosed you with TSD?"

"A friend."

"A counselor? Therapist? Family doctor?"

"She's a lawyer, actually."

A shadow of irritation flitted across the doctor's face, and Adhara explained.

"I went to her for a divorce, but she suggested I might need . . . help."

"Does your being here mean you agree with her?"

"No." It wasn't until she actually said it that she knew it was true. "I mean, I do need help, but not the kind she thinks. I do have a disorder, but it isn't imaginary. I'm not the same person I was before I transported."

"During which particular transport did this change take place?"

"The first one. Every one." Her jaw clamped shut. *What's the point? He won't understand.*

The rest of the session consisted of Dr. Sargo staring patiently at her as she fidgeted and sat in silence.

She left the office and turned away from the elevator to duck into the ladies' room. The building was relatively new, and the mirror toggled between reflective and camera. She leaned forward, switching her image back and forth. Her complexion was better than it had been, wasn't it? Or was makeup improving?

Footsteps clacked toward the door and Adhara hopped away from the mirror.

A vaguely familiar woman came in, glancing meaningfully between Adhara and the mirror.

"You didn't make a follow-up appointment," she said, falling into place as Dr. Sargo's receptionist.

"No, I didn't."

"Some people. . . ." She bent over so she could spy for feet in the stalls. When she reached into her jacket pocket, Adhara fleetingly wondered if what would come out would be a syringe filled with a mind-altering drug, like in one of the thrillers she had started reading three — no, four — transports ago.

The receptionist pulled out an old-fashioned paper business card, slid it into Adhara's hand and folded Adhara's fingers over it, as if it were contraband.

Adhara hated unfinished sentences. It was one of the things she found most irritating about Taavi these days. "Some people what?"

"Some people want a different kind of help. Please don't tell anybody I gave you this, but do pass it on, if you know of anybody else like you."

The receptionist slipped out of the room.

Infected by her air of intrigue, Adhara kept the card palmed until she had locked herself into her car.

Beside Ourselves - A support group for the Transported

A time, a date and an address had been scrawled under the single printed line.

~*~

She half-expected to have to give a secret knock or a password, but a bright-eyed woman opened the door at her approach.

"Adhara?"

"So they tell me."

The woman laughed. "You've come to the right place. Laila told us you might come. I've been watching for you. I'm Basht Kareem." She announced her name as if it were an accomplishment.

Basht led Adhara into an ordinary sitting room filled with ordinary people, except that each of them had an intensity most people lacked. Some looked hollow and grief-stricken, some looked sharply focused, some looked scorched with anger, but nobody looked complacent. Even the smug ones were *intensely* smug, aglow with self-satisfaction.

They were all, as she had gathered from the card, people who, unlike Jacinta, felt that "some micro-slippage" did matter. Some, like herself, had come looking for an answer — or, at least, for a question to ask. Some had found their answers and had come to share them.

Basht Kareem, it turned out, was an accomplishment. The woman who called herself that had been born under another name. Then she had stepped out of the transport station one day, convinced she was a different person. She had just walked away from her life, renamed herself, and stayed under government radar until she had been in residence long enough to claim deportation immunity. Which everyone thought very amusing, since her original self was a native-born citizen.

One of the men was an attorney who offered his services pro bono to anyone who wanted a divorce, citizenship application, name changes or wills.

Several people wanted wills. Lateral wills, they were called, in which one left all one's worldly goods to oneself. Many wealthy people had them, since many of them transported frequently and over long distances, and since many of them had relatives who had made nuisances of themselves by claiming that dis-materialization had killed the wealthy one in question, leaving them, the heirs, in ownership of the estate. No such suit had ever been upheld, but one never knew.

These people, though — the people at the meeting — wanted to will their estates to themselves under new names. It did no good for the lawyer to tell them that a legal name change would transfer ownership of any property automatically.

Had they always been so irrational? So unreasonable? So . . . weird?

She excused herself and hurried back to the car she no longer thought was beautiful and drove back to the home she knew she used to find slightly shabby. In the hall, she regarded herself in the mirror again. Didn't her hair have a slight curl to it? Wasn't it just a little bit darker? Just a little?

"Still at it?"

Taavi lounged in the doorway, drinking orange juice from the bottle. She never drank orange juice, so he was welcome to it.

"I'm not transporting anymore."

"Don't you have to, for your job?"

"I'll get Father Gephart to sign something for me. They'll put me on local. It'll be a salary cut."

"We won't be able to move into that new place in Northside."

"I don't care. Do you?"

He shook his head, vanished into the kitchen, and came back without the orange juice.

Standing close to her, peering down at her, he said, "I have only one question. Who are you, and what have you done with my wife?"

"That's two questions," she said, and laughed breathlessly. She felt giddy, the way she had felt when they first met, the way she hadn't in a long time.

"Do you still think you're a different person? I mean, really, *really* an actual different person?"

She wanted to say *No*, to hold onto this happiness, to not trigger the ill feeling that had grown up between them along with her unease.

"I do."

He stepped back, eyes hooded, then cocked his head.

"Would you say that again?"

"Say what again?"

"Say 'I do.' Adhara, will you marry me again?"

"What?"

"If you're a different person, let's get married again. I think you're still you, even if you're different. I love all the people you are and all the people you've ever been and ever will be. That's what love is, isn't it?"

Is it? Maybe it is.

"I will," she said. "I do." She did.

For the next two, written for Story A Day May, I pulled my prompt from my spomments, which is my word for spam comments people attempt to stick on my blog. They can be irritating, amusing, and downright puzzling.

Snow On The Screen

Emerson draped a muffler over himself and tied it under his control panel.

"Now, don't overdo." His wife, Sylvania, said the same thing every time he went out to shovel the walk. She added, as she had taken to doing the last few years, "Neither of us is getting any younger."

He didn't need her to tell him. The foil extensions on his rabbit-ear antennae ached whenever the weather changed. He was always losing his off-on knob and having to crawl all over the floor to find it, and his fine tuning knob had been gone for decades. Back when he was still in service, his boss had kept a pair of pliers up top, right behind the reproduction statue of End of the Trail.

That was before his blue/yellow color balance had blown.

Even then, the boss had moved him to the workshop and turned the saturation all the way down and watched the woodworking programs in black and white. Yeah, that was a boss! He had put up with the occasional snow on the screen, thumping Emerson on the head in a friendly sort of way to shake him back to full reception.

That was before this digital stuff. After that, there was no snow on the screen with faint sound and ghostly pictures that you could kind of follow until reception came back. With the digital, you either had reception or you didn't. And even then, you needed some kind of gizmo to translate the signals from digital to analog or some damn thing or other.

Emerson sighed and shoveled.

And the Missus was in the same shape. Sylvania had been a fine figure of a television in her prime. But times had caught up with both of them. Plenty of good years in them yet, but here they were, in forced retirement.

He reached the end of the walk and went in for a warm-up.

"Why don't you rest a bit before you do the drive?" Sylvania felt his back. "I think I can smell overheated circuits."

"That's your toast," he said, patting her hand. "I'm fine."

In the garage, he fitted the snowplow to his front and, conscious of the irony, clicked the remote to open the door.

The snowplow made short work of the driveway, and Sylvania's strong coffee was still perking through his wires.

What good does it do sitting around feeling sorry for yourself? At least we can still manage. Not like poor old Mrs. Ironing-Board, or the Pogo Sticks on the corner, or the Sony brothers who could only sit around bragging about what state-of-the-art transistor radios they used to be.

Sylvania was watching him from the picture window. He gave her a wave and a thumbs up, hitched his snowplow firmly around his middle, and went to see how many driveways he could clear before he wore out.

Other Earth, Other Stars

A WRITING PROMPT FROM THE SPAM FILE: TV fitted with a snowplow decided to go up and down the road and clear everybody's driveway

A Long Time Coming

"Mum! Mum!" Elgin stood on tiptoe, as if that would help a six-year-old see over the heads of adults. His mother, in the way of mothers, distinguished his voice through the hubbub and worked her way unerringly through the crowd.

He took her hand protectively. "You must stay close," he scolded. "I thought we'd lost you."

Mrs. Meachum knew her husband wouldn't be far from their son, and found him, exchanging fond glances with him over their boy's superior manner.

"We're quite lucky, Penelope," said Mr. Meachum. "We drew a location on Layer One! First on, first off, so we can accept first shift and be home for a good, wholesome English dinner and our favorite programmes on the telly."

"Hoorah!" Elgin had taken a great deal of teasing from his mates about his coming banishment to a diet of snails, and looked forward to rubbing their snouts in their error.

Mrs. Meachum smiled weakly. "I do wish we could find work in England. Commuting is so tiresome."

Elgin scoffed. "Oh, Mum! Imagine if we had to do it by road! The Channel Streamer is faster than driving from one side of London to the other." He said this as if they hadn't all read the brochures and contracts, hadn't all watched the recruitment video together, hadn't been discussing it endlessly for months. "And, since it rides above the water, it's unaffected by rough weather and the gyros won't let it tip or sink."

Together, the Meachums and the members of the surrounding crowd who had been enjoying Elgin's parroting of the video all said, "There in a flash, back in a flash. *Voila!*"

From somewhere high above, something that was programmed to sound like a steam whistle blew. The crowd on the dock cheered and threw confetti and streamers.

"They won't do that every day, will they?" Mrs. Meachum disapproved of untidiness.

A nearby man, heavy and wearing blue denim coveralls, said, "Oh, yes. Paid to, you know, by the Streamer company to make it all look like a jolly adventure."

"Silly," said Mrs. Meachum.

"I think it's rather nice," said a young woman — little more than a girl — with *Peg* stitched on the pocket of her blouse. "Almost like we're going on holiday, isn't it?"

"Dunno about you," said the heavy man, "but I've got ten long hours ahead of me over amongst the Froggies. Some holiday, eh?"

They all chuckled politely and let the subject slide.

~*~

Eleven hours later, Layer One First Shift disembarked in England. Ten hours of catering to English-speaking tourists who refused to learn French for the adults and ten hours of school, recess, and homework in the English workers' compound for their children had left them all exhausted.

"At least we did get home quickly," Mrs. Meachum conceded.

"It'll all get easier as we grow accustomed to it," Mr. Meachum consoled her with more hope than conviction.

"Bread and cheese for lunch?" Elgin was still outraged. "Mum, can I take my lunch tomorrow? Potted meat sandwich and a tin of fruit cocktail?"

"Of course, dear," said Mrs. Meachum.

Mr. Meachum clapped his son on the shoulder with fatherly pride. "That's the spirit," he said. "None of that nasty foreign muck for us, eh?"

"Snails, indeed!" said Mrs. Meachum, as she stepped thankfully onto good, honest, English soil.

A WRITING PROMPT FROM THE SPAM FILE: This has obviously been a long time coming, but given the economic conditions of many of the city. Although hiring a good moving company for your shipping needs is one way of mitigating the anxiety of moving overseas, there are other ways of ensuring smooth sailing for your international removal. And there are a large number of families who relocate from the UK to France almost daily. Seven layers are what the OSI model is built on and the counting usually begins from bottom to the top. The atmosphere around the docks is very festive for all.

Alien Worlds

Maybe there'll never be faster-than-light travel. Maybe we'll never find sentient life (that we can recognize and with which we can interact) on other planets. But that's no fun! What's interesting is imagining people like us somewhere and somewhen else.

"The Woman Who Wasn't A Shavetail" features a bit character from my novel SIDESHOW IN THE CEN-TER RING. The woman of the title is the main charac-ter from that novel, but the story is told by someone who was only in one scene, but insisted on having his own story.

The Woman Who Wasn't
A Shave-Tail

I was standing here, right in this very spot, when this bare-necked beggar, not old but not a kit, came up. He was yellow-orange — they're never anything but trouble — and obviously out of place in the big city. You know how these yokels are . . . well, I guess you don't, you being an off-worlder. They're either rough-looking or over-groomed; some of them use pomade to get that fur just so, you know? This fella was a little on the shaggy side. Nothing on — not a chestpack, not a purse-belt, nothing. Oh — he had a burlap pocket fastened to his fur with a couple of pinch-clips; it was up under his arm, where the hicks like to tuck them. Those evil city-slickers can't steal your alfalfa money if you clip it right up there under your arm, right?

"Go on, get out of here," I said. "You're blocking the table."

He looked around, but nobody was interested in jewelry and holy trinkets; this stuff I put outside usually grabs tourists, but this was off-season. He pulled out his pink slip — his status papers — to show me he was freehold — like I couldn't tell from his neck: no collar, you know? — as of the Release.

See, at the Release — comes every seven years — all slaves are freed. All slave records automatically roll over to freehold at the Central Registry.

—You're doing that face: that "slavery is evil" face you Terrans make. Excuse me, I don't mean to be rude, but it gets my back hairs up. Look at this — look at how they're standing on end back there. I hate that.

Our slaves get a signing fee — sometimes pretty hefty — in place of a salary. They have a union. No kidnapping allowed, like you people used to do. —Okay, okay, it was before your time. No offense meant, none taken, I hope.— Every seven years, they're all freed and either sign up again or don't.

"So you're free," I said to the beggar. "Congratulations."

"I need a place to spend the night, and some food."

"Why tell me? Look—" I pointed across the street. "There's a man with a brazier. Smell that spiced meat? He sells that to hungry people. And look over there—There's a sign in that window, 'Rooms to Let'."

"I don't have any money."

"Is that my problem?"

"Help me. Please." He held out his palms, like this, with the fingers spread. That's like a kit wanting to be picked up, it's that kind of asking. He was telling me he wasn't a man compared to me, that his universe revolved around me.

His palms were calloused but not cracked. He had done plenty of hard work on a long-term basis; had kept his pads medicated until they toughened up, a sure sign of a good worker. So what was he doing in the city, asking me for a handout?

Luck. I'm a very lucky fella. Oh, yes.

"Get out of here! All right, here's some money. Go

away."

He clutched the coins and said, "Thank you." I expected him to give me a grin and go try the act on somebody else, but he just stood there.

"No more," I said. "Move along, or I'll call the law."

He flashed a bitter look and said, "That's all the law is good for: rousting people who need help, but never helping them."

"So what do you want?" I had to ask, right? "You need money, go sell yourself. I notice your old master didn't re-negotiate for you."

"I'm in trouble. Well, I'm not in trouble, but. . . . I need help."

I didn't want to hear his sad story, but I could see he was going to tell it to me. Some people, you know you aren't going to get rid of so easy. I have a nephew like that. "Here," I said. "At least come in out of the way."

He followed me into the shop, which was almost as bright as the street. When your stock in trade is shiny stuff, it pays to have plenty of light on it. Back of the counter and behind a curtain, I keep a little room with a cot and a kettle.

He sank onto the floor like he'd been on his feet since his eyes opened. I gave him a mug of sweet cha and bag of dried fruit.

"Are you happy now?" I asked.

He shook his head.

"And you're going to tell me why."

"I'm from a village a little way upstream." (He meant up the Tammi, that river on the west side of town. Goes into the back country.) He stopped to stuff a cube of dried fruit into his mouth, then I had to wait while he tried to work his teeth out of the sticky mess without drooling all over himself.

When his mouth was clear enough, he gargled, "My name is Raj."

"Shahtsi," I said. We gave each other's noses perfunctory licks. His tongue left a trail of fruit sugar that dried and itched.

He went back to his story. "My youngest brother, Jimi, left home six months ago to come here, to Muimmea, to enter the Yolanbayt."

A Yolanbayt is like what you would call a monastery. My nephew used to be in one; he's a very holy fella, but he got bored or something, and came out.

"He never got there. When we didn't hear from him, we wrote to the Yolanbayt, but they hadn't seen him. We thought a rogue slaver might have waylaid him and taken his papers, bribed a Registrar to register him slave; but we weren't too worried about it, since it was nearly the Release. Father thought it might even do him good to see the rough side of the world for a few weeks. But the Release is past, and he still hasn't shown up."

He opened his pocket and took out a small strip of paper.

"Mother sent me this in a letter. Mother's the best cook in our village. Naturally, she was put in charge of the feast. It was supposed to start on the night of the Release and go on for fifty days. Everybody who was freed was supposed to come home for part of the celebration."

"I'm just assuming that all this has something to do with what you started to tell me."

He nodded and licked fruit gum off his fingers. "Mother opened a case of dried noodles a couple of weeks before the celebration — she wanted to make sure she hadn't been shorted — and she found this."

He handed me the slip of paper. I put on my spectacles

and read it.

Help. Prisoner, it said, in a kit-like scrawl. It was signed *Jimi*.

"He knew Mother was the festival cook," Raj said. "He managed to sneak that paper into the case that was set aside for our village, to let her know where he was. Since he hasn't come home, he must still be there."

I put my spectacles away, using that as a cover for cleaning the dried fruit paste off my nose. "Your mother told her local Registrar?"

Raj nodded. "The Registrar said she'd make an inquiry. A few days later, she said she'd heard from the factory: Jimi wasn't there."

"And you don't believe it."

"Neither does my mother. She says the Registrar doesn't believe it, either, but the Central Registry stands and falls on its paperwork, and there are no papers on a young slave named Jimi at that noodle factory."

"Well, there wouldn't be, would there, if they were keeping chained bodies?"

Chained bodies. That's pretty close to what you people used to do to each other. I'm sorry, but is it true, or isn't it? Highly illegal here, very big trouble if you're caught. If this factory was running chained bodies, they'd go as far as they had to to keep the secret.

"I can't push the law any harder," Raj said, "or the factory people might. . . . Jimi might. . . ."

I put a hand on his shoulder. "Let me call my nephew. He's a pretty smart fella."

~*~

Well, I should have known. The minute I looked up and saw that orange bumpkin blocking the sunlight, I should have known this whole thing was going to turn strange. Because my nephew came to the shop — Oh, yes, you can always count on Tosun to answer a call for help — but he had to bring her with him. Connie Phelan. I like Connie — don't get me wrong, Connie and I are like two kits in a kindle, but you never know what she'll decide to do.

"Hiya, Shahtsi," she says to me, with that big black-lipped grin of hers. Yeah, THE Connie Phelan. The Terran holo star. She lives here, on Marner. Yeah, she really looks like that. Accident with a cosmetic product, she said: patches of different colored skin and hair — black, tan, white. . . . When I first saw her, I thought she was a shave-tail.

—A shave-tail is one of us with the fur trimmed real close. Shave-tails hang around with Terrans and wear clothes. We don't think much of them, generally speaking.

So Tosun walks in with her behind him. My nephew is a good-looking fella, gray with black stripes, like me. You know how she looks — calico plus. She was wearing a black leather jumpsuit with the legs stopping just above her knees, black leather ruffles around the neck and wrists. She had diamond buckles on the toes of her black patent half-boots, and those gloves with the fingers cut out, also in black leather.

Tosun and I licked noses. Connie wiggled her multi-colored fingers at me.

Raj glanced from me to him to her and curled his lip. "I thought you said he was smart."

"I heard that." Connie showed him what his sneer might look like if it ate its vegetables and grew up big and strong. "If this half-grown rube calls me a shave-tail, I'm going to comb the hayseeds out of his hair with his teeth."

Tosun smiled reassuringly at Raj. "She's a Terran," he said. "She's a very nice person, really."

Connie snorted and sat on the cot. Probably afraid she'd get her clothes dirty, sitting on the floor with the rest of us.

"Aren't you working?" I asked. (—You watch her show? That's filmed right here in Muimmea.)

"Season hiatus. Why, Shahtsi?" She grinned again and said, "Think this would go better without me?"

"It would probably go safer without you."

"Uncle Shahtsi. . . ." Tosun thinks Connie is an Untutored Sage — a natural wise person. Natural wise mouth, maybe.

I sighed. "All right. Okay."

While I poured steaming mugs of cha for us all, Raj told them his story.

When he finished, Connie asked, "Where is this noodle factory?"

"Up Tammi River," Raj said, "past the Tammi Resort."

Tosun frowned. "Beyond Omata country. A kit would never make it home from there, even if he could escape."

Raj thumped his fist on the floor. "I have to get him out. I'll get some money. I'll buy some weapons. . . ."

My nephew shook his head. "Committing crimes of your own will only hurt your legal position. You would probably fail, and your attempt could be very dangerous for your brother."

"I have to get him out!" Raj repeated.

"We," said Connie, "have to get them all out."

"We?" I said. "All?"

"All the chained bodies. All of them."

See what I mean about her?

~*~

Tosun's mate, Tiph, was busy with their kits, an occupation of the deepest reverence, but she did some research for us.

Connie's mate was off-planet on some kind of business, or he'd have been in the thick of it, too. Connie rented a sailing boat for us — a yacht or a ketch or something. It was a boat. With a sail. She offered to pay me to close up shop for as long as this took; I didn't accept the money, but she offered.

So the four of us sailed up the Tammi to a bed-and-breakfast in Domba, this one-aazzi factory town where the noodles came from. We stopped at Tammi Resort along the way: Connie and Tosun know a couple of Registrars there.

Connie left the rest of us on the boat and came back with three pink slips and three very fancy neckbands. They all matched: silver mesh, with sapphires and pearls hanging from the lower edges. She plunked them down on the mess table, where we were all gathered for a council of war, like they were barbed wire and cockle-burrs.

"Robh and Bulfa say the Registrar in Domba is a rotten, graft-grabbing, underhanded sleaze bucket. Just the type who'd fudge papers and lie through his fangs. Nothing easier than to give Jimi another name, change his age a little, let the papers roll over to freehold, and claim he'd re-upped along with the rest of the happy workers. Ask me why."

"Why?" Tosun asked. He's very good-natured.

"Because, according to Tiph, the Star-Grain Noodle Company has a very thin profit margin, and it's getting thinner."

"This was a bad year for grain," Raj told us. "The sixth in a series of bad years, but this was the worst."

I cleared my throat pointedly. "If you're through with the farm report, could she go on?"

Raj ducked his head like he'd been hit. Country-bred: Tough body, thin skin.

"So," Connie continued, "I figure the factory's owner, Yoshe Scertz, shaved some expenses by buying slaves that fell off the back of a truck, if you know what I mean. Contraband. Stolen. The paperwork shows respectable signing fees, but she really just slipped the Registrar some graft and kept the money, but claims it as a business expense when the Empress' tax collectors ask for documentation. It's a small factory — just twelve workers — but twelve signing fees add up."

She leaned forward and directed a question to me. "Say your business depended on slave labor. Say your business wasn't doing so well. Now, say all your slaves were going to be freed, and you'd have to re-negotiate for them or buy new ones, with new signing fees going to each one. What would you do?"

"Sell before the freedom came," I said. "Naturally."

"Yoshe Scertz didn't. Didn't even try."

"She was afraid the slaves would tell the buyer what she'd done," Tosun guessed.

"Wouldn't that be nice?" Connie's smile twisted sardonically. "You have such a sweet clean mind. Sometimes I envy you."

"What — what do you think she's doing?" Raj had barely met Connie, but he already knew that asking what she thought was something you hesitate to do. Trainable.

"Well, first, she paid her crooked Registrar to do the fake roll-overs, then she recorded paying generous re-up fees. I'd be willing to bet she claimed all her slaves re-signed. She's looking decent on paper, but she doesn't have much profit left."

"Just a pocket full of cash she slipped out the back door," I said.

Connie nodded. "A perfect time for a devastating accidental fire, leaving no survivors."

Raj grasped at the table, his claws making faint scratches in its rough surface. "She would . . . burn my brother?"

"And the others. Then she takes her secret cash, takes the Empress' loss-of-livelihood bounty, and opens another business elsewhere."

"And the Registrar?" Tosun asked.

"Maybe he'd be happy with what he's got, just sit tight and wait for another scam to come along. Maybe he'd threaten to turn her in if she didn't keep paying. Or maybe she'd arrange for him to be inspecting the work environment when the fire broke out. Another tragic victim."

Raj edged away from Connie, looking at her out of the corners of his eyes. "How did you ever think of all that?"

Tosun smiled. "Only the brightest spirit can illuminate the darkest corners of the heart."

"Whatever," said Connie. "We go in, and we buy the woman out. With my money, of course. Safe and easy."

"But she can't afford to let chained bodies pass into somebody else's hands," I said.

"She can, if she thinks she's selling to somebody as low-down as she is. So that's what she has to think."

We all looked at Connie.

"What?" she asked.

~*~

Before we left the ship, she glued this stuff on her face — she learned how to do it from her make-up artist — made her look like a shave-tail with a muzzle job: Not quite Terran, not quite Marneri.

We met in the mess again, again with the slave-collars

glittering on the table.

"How do I look?" she asked.

"Disgusting," I told her. "I can hardly stand the sight of you."

"Perfect!"

"So you're a wealthy shave-tail and we're your slaves. Can we do this and go home?"

"Well, actually. . . ." Connie picked invisible lint off her crimson blouse. "I can't get too close to her, or she might spot the fakery." She handed a fancy collar to Tosun, and another to Raj. The third, she picked up and fastened around her own neck. "Besides, you're the businessman, O Master."

I booked all the available rooms at the River View Bed-and-Breakfast in Domba. I would have booked the whole place, but there was a honeymooning couple in the Love-Retreat Suite. Tosun got all misty-eyed over it, but I prayed to the Mother that they'd keep themselves to themselves.

The desk clerk wanted to make trouble over Connie — no shave-tails allowed — but she just stuck her muzzle in the air and let me handle it. That was probably the hardest part of the whole episode for her — keeping her mouth shut.

"You have a problem with one of my slaves?" I asked, very cold, as if he didn't have the right to breathe my air, let alone question my taste.

"We don't cater to them," he snipped.

"She isn't booking the rooms. I am. Tell me, Kit," (and I meant that to sting), "do you own this place?"

"No."

"Suppose you call the owner and say you just lost the

chance to fill the place because—"

"All right, you made your point. But she has to use the back door."

"I've used the back door in better joints than this," Connie muttered.

We pretended not to hear.

"What brings you to Domba?" The clerk used that phony voice that tells you he doesn't care, and you could say, "I came to blow the place to the twelve ends of Paradise," and he'd say, "Have a nice day."

"I'm looking for an out-of-the-way investment. Some place I can park some cash until it cools off, then pull it out again." I leaned closer. "Strictly legal, understand?"

He looked tickled furless to be on intimate terms with a wheeler-dealer like me.

"You look like a very smart fella," I said. "If you hear about a deal like that — and price is not a problem — you let me know. There'd be a finder's fee in it for you."

I peeled off one of the credit vouchers Connie had given me and slid it across the registration counter.

"I'll keep it in mind," the clerk said. "I surely will."

~*~

It wasn't quite dark when the visiphone tinkled in my room. We were all there, of course, playing cards to pass the time. The caller was a taffy-colored fella with white hands and a white blaze on his chest.

"Welcome to our humble village," he said, with a Muimmea accent that was too perfect to be real. "I have the privilege to be the Registrar in this district. My name is Chee Tamarie. I hope I can be of service to you while you're here."

"I fail to see how," I said, "but thank you for the offer."

I reached out, like I was about to turn off the 'phone.

"One moment, please!" He held up a hand, as if he could block me from the controls. "I understand you're looking for a long-term investment. Money no object?"

"I wouldn't say it's no object, but I'd pay above the Empress' evaluation of a business that suited me."

"If you're that interested. . . . I could pick you up tomorrow morning—"

"Late morning."

He smiled an oily smile. "Of course. Late morning. I know someone with a business she might be willing to let go, if the price is right."

"If the business is right, the price will be right. Located here in Domba?"

"Yes. A factory. The factory, actually." Chee laughed like a man trying to pretend he isn't part of what he's apologizing for. "Slave-staffed, entirely. Twelve just re-signed after the Release. There's . . . well . . . no difficulty, but. . . . It's a delicate matter." He winked.

"I know what 'delicate matter' means," I said, and didn't wink back. "I've dealt with 'delicate matters' before. I'm not afraid of 'delicate matters'."

He chuckled. "Good. Tomorrow, then."

"And make sure whatever you come to fetch me in has room for my slaves. Three of them."

"Is it really necessary—"

"Where I go, they go."

"The person you're going to see wants you to come alone."

Out of the 'phone's line of vision, Tosun slapped his chest, then Raj's, and made muscles.

"Two of them are bodyguards. I don't go anywhere

without them."

"Understandable. But the third? I hear she's a. . . ."

"She was a gift from a business associate. Never mind why I keep her close, but it isn't what you think, judging by the look on your face. In fact, I ought to send my fellas—"

"Sorry." he wiped his face clear of expression. "My mistake. You and three slaves. That won't be a problem."

"Fine. See you tomorrow."

I clicked off the 'phone.

Connie peeled away her false muzzle and rubbed her face. "At last! I don't know how you people stand these things."

Raj cocked his head. "But ours. . . ."

Connie snickered.

Raj turned to Tosun and said, "That show she's on; somebody else writes the comedy, right?"

I began to warm to the little fella.

~*~

The next day, Chee showed up just before mid-day with a closed carriage. It was drawn by half-a-dozen matched slaves — sleek fellas, all a sort of bluish-gray, all the same size and build. When Connie strutted out, they stared at her, then lowered their heads and snuck peeks.

I thought she was over-doing things a bit, but who am I to argue? She wore a typical shave-tail outfit: bright yellow plastic trousers, bright green short-sleeved shirt — it's possible she could have picked something that would have looked worse with the sapphires and pearls of her slave collar, but she had been working against time. She wore silver sunglasses with the frame of each eye shaped like a five-petaled flower, and shiny black close-toed shoes. She even stuck red-white-and-paisley scarves in the . . . you know . . . up here — where your females' lactation organs hang out all the time — excuse me, no offense, but it's . . . you know . . . alien. So she put scarves in there and let the edges show, so it would look like she was all stuffing up there, the way shave-tail females do. And you know how her hair is — all different patches? She made Tosun gather up each patch and tie a red ribbon around the end. She put gloss on her black lips. —Yes, they're really black, this was just gloss. She had gotten some false claws from somewhere, and stuck them on her fingers. She couldn't do anything with them on, but she said that was the point — she was a luxury model; she didn't have to do anything.

Chee rode inside with us, making chit-chat about the weather. He never once let his eyes rest on Connie, so maybe she was dressed right, after all.

~*~

The factory owner, Yoshe Scertz, was an overfed long-hair, brown with irregular black spots. She met us in her home, on the factory grounds. It was only two stories high, but covered with — what do you call it? — gingerbread; round towers on the front edges — no corners, of course, everything rounded.

Scertz led us into a dining room where a low table, with three pillows around it, was set for three.

"I thought we'd have a drink, to seal the bargain."

"You two," I said to Tosun and Raj. "Behind me." To Connie, I said, "Go over and inspect the factory for me. Be quick, but keep your eyes open."

"Can't that wait?" Scertz objected.

"Saves me time," I said. "If she says it's a good investment, it's a good investment. I don't even have to look."

Chee and Scertz exchanged glances. She said, "Chee, why don't you go with her? Show her around? Answer any questions she might have?"

Chee nodded.

"And Chee—" Scertz called, as he followed Connie out. He turned. "At a suitable distance, do I make myself clear? Don't touch her, don't stare at her. She is the property of my guest; treat her with respect. Respect, do you hear me?"

The Registrar nodded again, looking very sour, and left.

"I appreciate your looking out for my girl," I said to Scertz. "I didn't realize the trouble she'd cause out here in the wilds." Which was a lie, of course: Connie could cause trouble alone in a crypt. Dead.

When they got back, Connie gave me a big nod, with another nod to Raj. "Looks like a loser, and one of the slaves is just a kit, but it's perfect for what you want it for."

"Good enough," I said. "Let's do paper."

Chee fetched a stack of forms from a carved wooden chest. He laid them on the table near Scertz; she put a hand on them, her manicured claws extended. I got the message — here they were, but she wasn't ready to let them go.

"Chee told you there was . . . a special circumstance attached to this transaction," she said.

I nodded. "Something to do with the personnel, is what I gathered. Something shady with the slaves?"

Scertz's nose twitched, and her lips curled up in a tiny smile.

"It's a pleasure doing business with a man who doesn't need to have everything explained to him."

Chee shifted on his pillow, and I figured this was a not-so-subtle dig at the Registrar.

Scertz signed, I signed, I paid, and the business was

over.

Chee poured tall thin glasses of fermented cha for himself, Scertz, and me. He knocked his back like a pro and poured another.

"When can I take possession?" I asked.

"Next week, at the latest," Scertz answered.

Chee cut his eyes at Connie. "I'll still be in town. Available for business."

"Not now, Chee." Yoshe Scertz frowned.

"Formalities are over, aren't they?" He rose and crossed the room.

Scertz slapped the table. "Not in my house! Take it to town. Better yet, take it to Muimmea!" She turned to me and said, "He has a thing for shave-tails."

Before I could stop him, he grabbed Connie around the waist and gave her a big, slobbery lick on the nose. Licking latex — it must have tasted like the inside of a soccer ball.

Connie couldn't make a fist because of the fake claws, but she backhanded him a good one. He staggered back, almost falling over the table. I reached for him; he was too far away. He snatched Connie's hand and rubbed it, then went all the way up her arm. No fuzz, of course.

"She's not a shave-tail!"

Connie plucked off her claws, tossed them to the floor, and ripped off her muzzle. "Touch me again and see what happens."

I heard a click like I've never heard before.

Yoshe Scertz's voice was cold. "Nobody move."

Tosun said, "She has a gun."

"A what?" said Raj.

"It's a Terran weapon. Like a sling, but more deadly. Don't move."

My back hair rose. I could smell the tension in the room, and sensed my holy nephew resting at ease on his haunches.

Scertz said, "Chee, come over here." He did as he was told. "Now, we are all going to visit the factory. What bitter irony, that it should burn down just as it passed into new ownership, killing the new owner and his slaves. Here, Chee."

"She's giving him a gun," Tosun informed me; I was taking Scertz very seriously — I hadn't moved, not even my eyes.

"Stand up," Scertz said. "Chee, go in front of them. I'll bring up the rear."

Single file, we passed through the entry and out into the sunlight. Somewhere, someone had put a massive amount of fertilizer on a field. That good, fresh, clean country air.

—Yeah, that's really what I thought about. My first thought, when my brain started to work after the panic. My second thought was how I could kill Connie before Scertz and Chee got a chance. Of course, Connie would have had a point, thinking the same thing about me; after all, she wasn't the one who had called me with this mess. Then I thought how Connie and I could both kill Raj.

We were half-way to the factory when I heard a loud, fast buzz, then another, then a pair of TUNKs. Scertz sighed as she went down, but Chee collapsed without a sound.

Connie did that shriek and victory dance she does on the show when she puts one over on somebody. And from out of the bushes stepped the honeymooning couple from our bed-and-breakfast, each holding a government-issue sling.

"Shahtsi, Tosun, Raj," Connie said, "I'd like you to meet two of the Empress' finest. I called them from Tammi Resort and arranged for them to meet us in Domba. I was going to send them in to make the arrest as soon as we had the papers signed, but this is so much more satisfying, isn't it? Don't you just love the sound of justice bouncing off a skull?"

~*~

So that's what happened. I signed the factory over to Connie, she freed the bodies and sent young Jimi home — sent an armed escort to bring him to the Yolanbayt, when he was ready to try again. Some of the slaves actually offered to re-sign for her, but she wouldn't have it. Freehold or nothing, she said. She put some money into the place, and it's making a nice profit.

Raj? He should have stayed in the sticks, but he came back to Muimmea with his little brother. He wouldn't have been a bad beggar, but NOOO, he wanted a real job. Yes, he found one. Yes, he likes it. Seems to, anyway. He'll be back any minute; you can ask him yourself. So he's yellow-orange — By the Mother's grace, I don't judge people by the color of their fur. No offense.

Demon Ozone

A little girl with ringlets blue
And eyes of deepest gold
Approached the noisesome space canteen
And shivered with the cold.

She pulled a rag of green lamé
About her shoulders thin.
She pushed aside the swinging door
And then the child went in.

What sights are these to greet the eyes
Of one of tender years!
What sounds are these, from ev'ry side,
To fall on tender ears!

The worthless of a hundred worlds
Were crowding 'round the taps
Or seated at the tables dim
With girls upon their laps.

So, in amongst the revelers,
The gold-eyed urchin came

Until she reached a drunken man
Intent upon a game.

His hair had faded to pastel,
His eyes were shot with black.
The infant raised her tiny hand
And touched him on the back.

"Oh, father, dear," the child then said,
In accents mild and sweet,
"Please come back home. Mamma is ill,
And nothing's there to eat."

His eyes filled with repentant tears,
He fell upon his knees.
"And would you have me back?" he cried.
His daughter answered, "Please."

Oh, keeper of the space canteen,
Dispensing potions wild,
Pray God for grace, and think upon
The little Spaceman's Child!

Sanctuary

Brinna and Jamal threaded the dark, narrow streets, lit only by the candles and firelight from the buildings they passed.

As the building they sought swam into view through the gloom, Brinna gasped and said, "I forgot the password!"

"I didn't. Don't worry, Sweetheart."

Jamal winked at her and knocked at the door.

A peephole slid open. Jamal spoke the password and a proboscis poked out through the circle. The young people raised their free hands for the proboscis to explore.

"Too young, Soft Ones," a voice squeaked from the other side of the door.

"Our birthdays are tomorrow," Jamal wheedled. "Mine is in two hours and Brinna's is in seven."

"Is close," the voice admitted. The proboscis withdrew and the peephole clacked shut.

They stood in the growing chill.

The peephole snapped open again.

"No until tomorrow."

"But you don't understand! Our families cast us out for declaring our heartbond before time. We have nowhere to go!"

Clack!

A flake of white fell, then twenty, then icy wetness descended in a million relentless kisses.

Jamal pounded on the door. "A blizzard is coming! It's snowing! It's just a few hours! *Please!*"

Brinna pulled her cloak more tightly around her. "Let's ask for shelter somewhere else. Surely, *somebody* will take us in."

But the first place would not, nor the second, nor the third. They worked their way down one side of the street and back toward their original destination, growing colder and wetter and more exhausted. Before they heard their last refusal, the bell in the clocktower tolled the hour twice.

"It's your birthday," Brinna said. "Blessings, Beloved! *You* can go in."

"Not without you."

He wrapped her in his cloak as well as hers. Shivering in his shirtsleeves, he went back around, giving his new age. Always, he was welcomed but his betrothed was not. Always, he refused the welcome, then requested and received a handful of kindling or a stick of wood. He kept himself warm by running these back to the door where Brinna arranged the wood and sheltered it from the snow.

At last, he took his tinderbox and struck a spark that caught and spread.

The peephole flapped open and an eyestalk protruded, then jerked back at the heat of the rising flames. The door swung wide and a bucket of water doused their fire.

An extremely cross grachnid motioned them inside. By the orange coloration, she was a female of the highest caste they'd ever seen.

"Few hours, more or less, what matters?" She motioned for others of lower caste to take Brinna's and Jamal's cloaks.

"Welcome to grachnid embassy. Hold hands. Now you married by grachnid law. Congratulations. Stay here until young one is old enough to count with your people. Happy? Follow that one to a warm room. Will be food."

Brinna and Jamal tried to thank her, but the Ambassador only walked away.

Before she closed the sphincter to her office, she said, "Try not burn place down, agreed?"

Mixed Metaphor

A bunch of us clones were lapping it up
On Laredo's second moon.
We were there with Dan,
      Our parent-man,
And we'd cowed the whole saloon.

Now, Death-Ray Dan was a western buff,
And he dressed himself like that—
Nine tough galoots,
      Eight leisure suits,
One cowboy, complete with hat.

Dan was with Miss Belle LaFleur,
A gal he thought he owned.
She was quite a dish
      And she made us wish
That *she* was multi-cloned.

The door swung wide and a man stepped in
Dressed just like Death-Ray Dan
With the mask and hat
      And the stranger sat
And faced Dan man-to-man.

"This town is mine," he said to Dan.
"It's mine by fist and gun.
I got eight boys
      That'll make these toys
Of yours turn tail and run."

"Well, trot 'em out!" Dan growled. Sez Dan,
"Let's see you back your bluff!"
Us clones spread out
      'Cause there weren't a doubt
This guy was plenty tough.

His clones came in when he told 'em to,
And we blamed it on the booze:
For every cuss
      Looked just like us —
Not a clue to whose were whose.

Dan dropped his jaw. The stranger laughed
And threw aside his mask.
Dan said, "But how — "
      Said the stranger, "Now,
You very well might ask."

"Us two was twins," the stranger said,
"And still are, to this day.
Mom changed her genes
      And, to save bad scenes,
Dad went his sep'rate way.

"Each took a twin and settled down
And put the past aside

Other Earth, Other Stars

But the story true
      Dad — Mom, to you—
Told just before he died."

So Dan and his twin caught up on the life
They'd never shared before.
The rest of us drank
      Till we shivered and sank,
The clones on the barroom floor.

Independence

"Learning to drive seems difficult at first," Kkakk said, "but you'll soon get the hang of it, and then it'll be second nature to you."

Akkooo blinked in acknowledgment of his elder's wisdom, but omitted the half-blink that would have meant he accepted and agreed with the statement.

He wasn't at all certain he wanted to drive, but all his friends did, and his caregivers had made it plain they looked forward to his learning. It was putting a strain on his social life and his consortium relationships, his only being able to swim as far as his physical limit without someone else giving him a lift.

"I've been watching Bikkkk," he said, flushing when Kkakk waved in approval. They had both mounted the twofer jet, Akkooo in the driver's position for the first time in his life.

It would actually be easier, once he got his license, because he wouldn't be able to afford a twofer for, like, ever, so he'd be driving the smaller, more maneuverable single.

"Um. . . ." *Is this rude?* "Did you already check for barnacles and seaweed?"

Kkakk waved again. "I did. Good question! Glad to see Bikkkk knows his jet safety procedures."

"He always checks the seashield for cracks, too."

"Right. Everything in order?"

"Yes, Elder."

"Then we're ready to go."

Akkooo touched the starter. The motor hissed and bubbled to life. His beak clacked involuntarily and he leaked —just a little— ink with his anxiety. Colors played up and down his tentacles.

Nothing to be nervous about.

He faced stiffly sideways, one eye pointed ahead and the other behind. Prime tentacle on the brake, secondary on the speed; two backmost on steering; leftside and rightside curled around the braces to hold himself in place, and the final two free for emergencies.

Kkakk said, "Now ease forward on your speed while you lift. *Don't* hold the brake at the same time! That's it. Gently. . . ."

Akkooo was sure Bikkkk rose faster than this, but he didn't want to look like a squirt-tail, so he went as slowly as he could without killing the engine.

"Now, forward. Slowly, if you please."

I could propel myself faster than this!

"You're thinking you could propel yourself faster than this," said Kkakk, nearly causing Akkooo to clip the edge of a coral shelf. "And I'm sure you'll go faster, once you're trained. For now, let's just get used to the controls, shall we?"

They spent the entire day navigating the sea bottom, and even took the jet up into the middle reaches and opened her up to her full speed, sending out blasts of subsonic waves to warn the self-propelled of their coming.

When they ended at Akkooo's consortium, he set the twofer down with scarcely a bump.

"Very good," said Kkakk. "Two more sessions will probably do it." He waved all his tentacles at Akkooo's caregivers to let them know how well their fledgeling had done.

They invited him to stay for supper, but Kkakk declined.

"Our little larva is growing up," Akkooo's matron said. Akkooo tried not to change to match her color, but he was just too tired and happy. He gave up and relaxed into harmony.

All the other stories in this collection have appeared elsewhere. The following one is new.

I love doing research, and I got to do some on this one. Parthenogenesis is a real thing.

Leaving the Turtle

I was winning, as usual, at unarmed combat practice — the women of our bloodline against the women of Tam's — when the hut from Home appeared from the sky. The shuttle, I mean. I'm told the word is shuttle, although a shuttle is something you use to weave, not something you use to hold people. But I stand on my talents as a trader, a fighter and a linguist, so I'll use the proper word, silly as it is.

The sunlight flashing from it caught our attention first, before we felt the wind it pushed aside as it neared the ground. By the time it eased to a landing in the center of our settlement, we were all clustered at the meeting house, watching.

The Babas — our ten oldest, drapes hanging slackly across their sagging breasts, leg-drapes covering their skinny shanks — ranged themselves in a line between us and the shuttle. The Babas are spiteful old hags, stuck somewhere between the golden past and the "decadent" present. They're also my own personal nemesis individually and as a whole, but they don't lack courage.

"It's from Earth," said SharShar na Bal, oldest of the Babas. "They've come at last." Her smile was not a sweet one as she cut her eyes toward the north gate and the native village that lay beyond it.

She dispatched people to bar all five gates, others to prepare food and to freshen up an empty family hut for our visitors. There were certainly plenty of empty huts available — and more, every generation. She kept me by her in case I was needed to communicate with the newcomers. Besides, it was convenient having me at her elbow instead of sending for me when she wanted to make me miserable. I adjusted my loincloth and untied my drape from its binding of my breasts for combat.

The shuttle was about the size of a family hut, and about the same height, with stilts shorter and thicker than we used. It gleamed like metal, though not even the Babas were old enough to have ever seen anything that big made entirely out of metal.

The shuttle landed, made some settling noises, and sat silent. We stood and watched it.

"Should we speak first?" I asked at last.

SharShar na Bal twitched and said, "BranDal na Cam is always so impatient." She meant me — I come from First Mother Bran, my mother was Dal, and my name is Cam. "Very well, then, go speak."

Hypocrite. She would have waited until she grew roots before she spoke first, but I'd given her an opening and she'd taken it.

I walked closer to the shuttle and said, in the language of Earth our First Mothers had brought with them and passed down to us, "Welcome to Peace. We remember Earth. Welcome, Sisters."

I looked back at Bal, who gave me a grudging nod.

A hatch opened in the side of the shuttle, and a ramp unfolded. A figure came down. A figure with thick facial hair on . . . *his* . . . chin and upper lip. A figure with no breasts. A male. A *human* male.

Behind me, there was a soft wave of nervous laughter and murmurs.

A wave of relief followed, as two people came after him. The three were dressed alike in trousers and shirts, as our First Mothers dressed, according to the stories. Naturally, they would send the male out first, to make sure it was safe for people.

They looked like none of us. Of course, we knew there were Mothers other than ours, and that not all of the bloodlines our Mothers had brought here had survived — we knew there were people who didn't look like us. It was strange, though, after seeing the same faces for so long, to see new ones. I thought the new people were very exotic and very beautiful.

"Welcome," I said again. "Welcome to Peace."

The man and the people smiled, and the man held out his hand to me. This is why Bal doesn't just go ahead and exile me for what she calls my "bad attitude"— she enjoys watching me forced to interact with males.

I took his hand and held it, as one does a frightened child's. It was soft; the hand of one who does little manual labor. The stories handed down to us told of machines that did the hard work, but they told us little of the differences between the statuses of male and female on Earth. The native females on this planet did the harder work, yet had the lower status. Was it the same on Earth, as some of our people believed? Well, it wasn't so in this compound, there was no question about that.

"Be silent and stand still," I told him. "Don't touch anything. The people who brought you are our guests. A safe place will be set aside for you."

He looked puzzled. "I am Captain—"

I dropped his hand and walked past him to the people.

One of them gestured to the male and said, "This is Captain Pablo Huertos of the Terran Confederation ship *Carter*. I am Dr. Barbara Gilliam and this is Dr. Chandra Padi of the Xenoarcheology Institute."

Their speech was degraded from the Earth language we had preserved, but understandable. Perhaps the man hadn't understood my directions. That would explain his blatant disobedience.

"I apologize," I said to the woman. "I should have spoken to you and had you relay what I said to that man. Tell him to be silent and stand still and not to touch anything."

"I heard you," the man said.

I smiled at the people. "Will you come meet our leaders?"

The woman who had spoken before said. "We'd be delighted. But why do you ignore Captain Huertos?" She didn't sound angry, just curious.

The other woman, who had been observing the crowd behind me, said, "Where are your men?"

"What do they say?" SharShar na Bal demanded, irritated that her hearing couldn't follow our exchange.

I faced the Babas. I kept my face as expressionless as I could as I said, "They say this man has a name. They want to know why I don't treat him like a person. They want to know where our men are."

Everyone laughed, some a little uneasily because they hardly understood what I was saying.

Harshly, SharShar na Bal said, "Tell them we have no men."

"We have no men," I said.

The woman who had asked about our men said, "You're still parthenogenetic."

"Still what?" I asked.

"You still reproduce without males."

"What did she say?" asked Bal, and I translated, emphasizing the word "still" and straining to keep an evil grin off my face.

One of the other Babas, BrenCar na Den sniffed haughtily and said, "The natives have males. *People* don't."

"Interesting," the Earth person said, pressing buttons on a small device.

~*~

After some confusion and questioning about their foremothers, we decided to call the people NolaSara na Barbara and GuriChaitra na Chandra. The man, we just called the Traveler. It was as good a reference as any, for a man. Barbara and Chandra continued to treat him with respect, but they referred to him as Traveler when they spoke to us.

It pleased the Babas to pretend they didn't completely understand the visitors' patois, but the rest of us caught on to it fairly quickly — it wasn't all that different from ours.

"The Lost Colony!" Barbara said. "You should have heard them cheer on the ship and back at mission control on Earth. When we mounted this expedition, our most ambitious hope was to find enough traces of the colony here to theorize what had happened to it. And we find you."

The Babas had given them permission to study us and send their findings back to the Home Planet. So far, they had told us very little about the history we had missed in the past 200 years, saying they didn't want to contaminate their study.

~*~

As far as the Babas were concerned, I was already contaminated, so I was given the task of taking them to the Bowl of the Mothers and showing them what was left of the Crippling and the Destruction.

The strangers — even the man — had Earth weapons, probably better than the ones the First Mothers had brought with them, but the natives (supposing we met any) wouldn't know what they were. It's easier and safer to *look* dangerous than it is to *be* dangerous but *look* weak. We supplied the people with cudgels, since they didn't know how to use bows and arrows. the Traveler asked Barbara to ask me if he could have a slingshot, and I permitted it.

"Tell the Traveler he may speak directly to BranDal na Cam," Den, the sniffing Baba, said. "If she can speak to native males, surely she can speak to one from Earth."

"Cam does her job," Bal surprised me by saying.

The twist on Den's lips said, "That is no recommendation," but she said nothing.

~*~

There were no natives in sight as we crossed the grassy plains to the Bowl — the crater where the First Mothers had made their tragic landing.

We nodded to the children and barren people who kept our goats and sheep near the gate. It had been many long years since the natives had raided us, and one benefit of their having driven off large game was that large predators had followed. Still, flocks needed tending. As a barren woman, that would have been one of my jobs, when I wasn't on a trading expedition to the nearest native settlement, but it stands to reason that more empty wombs mean fewer children, and the fewer children we had to tend flocks, the more barren women we had for the jobs. Not a happy equation.

When we were past the paddocks, the Traveler scooped up a pocketful of pebbles from the pathway and practiced with the slingshot. He was a very poor hand, to begin with, but improved quickly. Then it was "Watch me hit this" and "Watch me hit that" until I told him to put it away and let the people talk uninterrupted.

"Where do the natives come from?" Chandra asked. "This was supposed to have been an uninhabited planet."

"Their origin story says they were born from the belly of the world," I said. "We think they may have been so few and so primitive — cave dwellers, then and now — the Earth scans didn't pick them up. When they showed up and settled down and our people were forced to learn their language and deal with them, they said they came from a mating of the world and the sun. The sun comes up in that direction," I pointed, "so that's probably where they migrated from. Since then, their men have killed or driven off all the large game and any of our stock they could catch. They're hunters and gatherers, mainly, but they produce good tools and cloth."

"What does *your* origin story say?" the Traveler asked.

"We don't have an 'origin story'. We have a history."

"Of course."

Barbara had her transmitting device out. "Tell it," she said. "What happened to the colony? Start at the beginning — Where do you come from?"

"We come from Earth, of course! We were genetically engineered to be strong and intelligent and to reproduce without males. What did you call it?"

"Parthenogenetic."

"That way, all of the colonists could reproduce, not just some of them. We would multiply and subdue the planet and make it ready for softer Earth people to follow us. But something went wrong with the landing, and the ship crashed. Some of the Mothers were killed. The ship was damaged. They couldn't even tell Earth what had happened."

Between one second and another, three native males were suddenly there, just outside the treeline, within shouting distance. They were no taller than one of our 13-year-olds but they carried bows and arrows and had knives strapped at their waists. They wore tunics and leggings made of animal skin. They braided their long yellow hair and beards and moustaches, working different colors of clay into the braids as decoration and camouflage. These three were obviously lookouts or poachers, their native purple tinge darkened almost to black by the sun.

We all stopped. Traveler slapped at his sides, unsure whether to draw his own weapon or the slingshot. I put down my bow and spread my arms for calm.

"I count three of them," Barbara whispered to Chandra. "How many do you see?"

"Three."

"If you see three," I said, "there are six. They want us to think we have the advantage."

"Are they hostile?" Barbara dropped her cudgel on her own foot, said a word that was probably improper, but didn't move to pick the club up.

"Not really," I said. "Just tricky."

The natives — the ones we could see — put down their weapons and spread their arms to agree to a parley, opening their three-fingered hands wide, to show they were empty.

I shouted a word of greeting in their language.

"Something came softly from the sky," one of them, whose nose was clay-whitened, said. "None of you were hurt, we hope?"

"Some of our relatives from the stars have come to visit, as we always said they would."

The natives made furtive hand-signals, under the impression I hadn't figured out their "secret" language. One of them wanted to run for reinforcements and one wanted to kill us immediately. I needed to stop this sort of thing before it got started.

"There are many of them," I said. "They live in a giant hut high above the trees and only sent a few in a little hut down here. They have great magic, and the ones in the hut above are watching us now."

The natives ducked and glared at the sky, easing back under the edge of the canopy.

"Will they take our planet back to Earth?" White-nose asked.

". . .No," I said. *No wonder they wanted to kill us.* "They will leave our planet where it is."

"Will they take *you* back to Earth?"

Oh, don't you hope so? "No. They will leave us where we are, too." . . .At least, I assumed they would. I suddenly flamed with curiosity to see Earth, or at least to see something besides the land within and close to our fortifications, large as that was.

The natives blended into the shadows again and appeared to be gone.

"Some of them are watching us," I said, "and some have gone back to tell their head man about you."

"They appeared to be male," said Barbara, who had transmitted everything. "Are they?"

"Those were," I said. "They have males *and* people, but the males have all of the power. They say that's why—"

After a moment, Chandra asked, "That's why what?"

"There is the Bowl," I said.

The Bowl rose from the grassland in a rocky rim. Over the years, our people had fashioned steps along and up the outside and many sets of steps and ledges on the inside.

When we reached the rim, we stopped. Barbara swept the panorama with her transmitter. Below us was the crater, the bottom thickly carpeted with wildflowers except for the large firepit in the center. The inner walls were honeycombed with niches, some empty, some holding pottery urns.

"The First Mothers salvaged what they could from the Crippling of the ship," I said. "Seed and seedlings, food supplies, some livestock, a few weapons, some agricultural equipment, some building equipment and materials. Not much, really. They had to survive on what was here, almost from the first. Fortunately, we were bred to be resourceful. Then came the Destruction."

For a moment, I couldn't speak. We were taught the history, but sometimes it was more than just a story to me. Sometimes I could feel the despair and sorrow of that blow.

"They say a big stone fell from the sky," I said. "No one is alive who saw it, but the Babas remember people who did. It crushed what was left of the ship and everyone in it. Many First Mothers died that day. Many of their bloodline died. Their bodies lie somewhere under the stone, under the ground."

"And the pots in the wall?" Chandra asked.

"This is where we honor our dead. We join the First Mothers here. Most of us."

"Why not all?" Barbara asked.

"One reason or another." I looked back toward the fortifications and saw the herders chivvying the flocks in for the evening milking. "It's time to go back. We'll have a feast tonight, in your honor. Are you sure you have enough of your special food to share? If not, we understand."

They had brought bars of concentrated food and had been generous enough to give us some. One of the children had been bad-mannered enough to ask them to bring some to the feast, but our embarrassment was tempered by delight when they assured us, as they assured me now, they were happy to oblige.

~*~

It was a fine feast: Besides the visitors' food bars, we had roast lamb, spiced goat, yams, onions, flatbread, and a native fruit that was sweet and tender and juicy. And *miluk*, of course. *Miluk* was what we called goat's milk fermented and sweetened with honey. It tasted so good and mild, and it was so very potent. We diluted the visitors' as we did the children's, but nobody diluted the Babas'.

They were irritated, to begin with, to have to seat a male at their table and, because they still affected not to understand the visitors, to have me there as well. The Traveler offered to sit at a small table nearby, where he could still listen but not offend our taboos. That irritated them even more.

"Natives have 'taboos'," SharShar na Bal said. "Of course, our visitors must be seated with honor."

"Just not named," Traveler said.

"Can you explain that to us?" Barbara asked, in that placidly curious way she had.

"You tell her," Den said to me. "You don't mind speaking of such things."

My evening could only get worse from here.

"We were made to reproduce without males," I said, putting it as bluntly as I knew how. "Males aren't necessary to us. We've seen the native males, and we understand why we were made the way we were. The native males are aggressive. They attack the weak. They abuse their women. They take all the power for themselves. They're all bad. All of them. Completely and without exception. Any male of any kind is nothing but bad, even our own."

"We have none!" BrenCar na Den growled.

"Oh, that's right," I said. "We have no males. Males don't deserve to be treated with respect. They don't deserve to live. They don't deserve to die with honor."

The whole table had fallen silent.

"You've insulted our guest," Den said, stiffly.

I had done more than that, but she couldn't reprimand me for it without drawing attention to it.

"I apologize," I said to the Traveler. He nodded, looking thoughtful. I must have had a little too much *miluk*, because I turned to Barbara and said, "What did you mean, we *still* reproduce without males? Were we supposed to start bearing males? Mating with them?"

BrenCar na Den had apparently had too much, too, because she sniffed and said, "Perhaps Cam is eager to try this new method of reproduction?"

SharShar na Bal rapped on the table with a knuckle. "That's quite enough. This is not the time or place to speak of such things."

My heart both leapt and broke at her words. This was something I hadn't thought of — that the Earth people, with their respected male Captain, would weaken the Babas' barricade of silence.

"When?" I said. "When will we speak of them?"

The other Babas muttered to one another, discomfort souring into anger.

SharShar na Bal said, "Cam, you may be excused from the table."

"You need me to translate—"

BrenCar na Den, whose eyes were nearly crossed with drink and whose cheeks were bright with rage, said, "Unnatural woman! Treasure men? Bear men? Mate with men? What next—goats? Why don't you try it first, BranDal na Cam, and tell us how you like it? Tell us how it's done, you, who know so much better than your elders."

"We will make do without you, BranDal na Cam," Bal said. "You will sleep in The Turtle tonight."

~*~

The Turtle was a round dome, four feet of its interior height below the soil. A hatch in its side opened onto stairs leading down to the floor. It was made of metal, a construct of the First Mothers, where they had germinated seeds and studied native flora and fauna, to see what was safe for us to eat. After the Destruction, nothing in it that went far wrong could be repaired, and its purpose changed. It became a place of enforced isolation.

I spent a lot of time here. I hated it. It felt unnatural, being inside metal, being in the ground, rather than being in scented wood and rustling reeds on stilts to catch the breeze. I missed the family hut, with my grandmother, mother, sisters too young to reproduce and the aunts and grown sisters who, like me, had never reproduced. Worse than that, I hated being stuck in this dead shell, this casing that used to be filled with future and promise, and now held nothing but the remains of the past. It reminded me of the Bowl of the

Mothers. Sleeping here was like sleeping with ghosts.

I did sleep, though, but was wakened by a hand at the hatch. They say The Turtle had once had mechanical power, but now the hatch was worked by manual controls, and had to be opened once a day to freshen the air. My sisters had had lots of practice, bringing me food and water during my stays, but whoever was working the lock now was fumbling.

I just *knew* the hand on the lock was the Traveler's and that the Babas had sent him. They had drunk even more after I had left, I had no doubt, and BrenCar na Den never let go of a thought, assuming one found its way into her skull. If I thought males were the same as people, and that people were supposed to mate with males, it would strike them as only fitting that I should be the subject of the experiment.

It didn't strike *me* that way.

The space between the backs of the steps and the wall was enclosed to contain some of The Turtle's long-useless mechanisms. I flattened myself against one of those walls and waited for Traveler's thick fingers to manage the clip and slide the panel aside.

The door opened. Fresh air and light burst into my prison, partly blocked by the Traveler's big male body. I felt my nose wrinkle in distaste.

"BranDal na Cam?" he called, in that deep rumble that made me think of rockslides. "BranDal na Cam? Cam?"

His heavy feet *tonged* on the metal steps as he eased down into the candle light. When he was far enough down, I reached around and jabbed the backs of both his knees.

"Ow! Ugh! Crap!" He tumbled to the floor, face down, disoriented and probably wondering, as I was, how badly he was hurt.

I straddled him and sat on his back, hard enough to drive some of the wind out of him. I whipped the drape from my breasts and looped it around his neck, pulling it tight enough to raise his head from the floor.

"I hope you don't think you came here to rape me," I said.

"Nuh-nuh. . . ."

"Death before dishonor," I said. "And when I say, 'death', I'm not talking about mine."

"Nuh," he said.

Now I had to decide what to do with him. I couldn't kill him. I couldn't just sit there, throttling him for the rest of my life. I supposed I'd have to release him and hope he didn't get any unpleasant ideas.

I let his head drop with a *clunk* and draped my breasts again. Rising, I adjusted my loin wrap and, giving his hip a little admonitory kick with my sandal, I moved away from him.

He rolled over slowly and sat up, knees drawn to his chest, and rubbed that big knob on the front of his neck. His face was bleeding in a couple of places from his fall. He'd probably have some bruises, too. I'd be doing more time in The Turtle for showing disrespect to a visitor, I had no doubt, but sometimes you have to make a point.

"Did the Babas send you after me?" I asked.

"That one that sniffs made some suggestions. But I didn't take her seriously. I think she was drunk. And I don't think she likes you very much." Sullenly, he reached into a pocket of his shirt and pulled out a silver-wrapped bar. "I brought you something to eat."

I held out my hands and he tossed it to me. It was

delicious: full of fat and salt, although they said it was bland, compared to real Earth food.

He shook his head as he watched me savor it. "I can't believe you *enjoy* that drek."

"Well, we do," I said. "But I still won't conjugate with you."

He gave me a look I was coming to know. It meant he was annoyed but curious.

"Do you even know what that word means?" he asked. "Do you know what the word 'rape' means?"

"It's what animals and natives do to make babies," I said. "Rape is when they don't want to, and conjugation is when they do."

"Look," the Traveler said, hauling himself gingerly up onto a step, "believe it or not, I want to neither conjugate nor rape you."

"Conjugate *with*," I corrected him.

"What would the Babas do if we pretended we did it? If we told them we did, although we wouldn't, really?"

I stopped eating for a moment to think about that. "*Lie? To the Babas?*" I thought of them, drapes hanging slackly across their sagging breasts, eyes boring holes through everything. Defy them, yes, deceive them, yes, but lie to their faces? The prospect charmed me, but I couldn't imagine it.

The Traveler ran a hand through his hair.

"I'm picking up some notions," he said. "Barbara and Chandra think we should wait until we're more accepted — until *they're* more accepted — to find out what's what, but I. . . ." He took a small cloth out of his back pocket and wiped the blood from his face. After inspecting the result, he said, "When we first landed, you said a safe place would be made for me. Am I in danger? Because I'm male? I can go back to the ship and send another researcher of the 'correct' gender."

"You're not in danger. Unless you try to—"

"I'm not going to! What is *up* with you people?"

I finished the bar, wadded up the wrapper and popped it in my mouth, savoring it as it reacted to my saliva and dissolved in a burst of sweetness.

"What is it?" he insisted. "If anybody is going to tell me, it would be you."

"We were engineered to reproduce without males. You know that." I heard the bitterness in my voice as I said, "Den — the sniffer — said it: Males are unnatural. Inhuman."

"I think you don't believe that," the Traveler said. "I think your duties as a trader and translater gives you the chance to see all kinds of native males."

I shrugged. I didn't want him to go on thinking and guessing. At the same time, I was so tired of being the only one who hated what we had become.

The Traveler said, "There's more, isn't there?"

"No," I said, at last. "There's no more."

He thought, then said, "You know the colony was supposed to start producing males. Did that not happen? Is that why there are so many empty huts?"

I said nothing.

Impatiently, the Traveler said, "Are you making this a guessing game? In your memory, or in any stories or rumors you've heard, did this colony ever have any males in it?"

"We never had men. We never did." After a moment, feeling as if I were lancing a boil, I said, "We never had *men*."

We sat in silence a moment, then he said, "Oh, my God."

I didn't look at him as I said, "They say that for a long time, there was plenty of food and the First Mothers' machines made work lighter than it is now. All the First Mothers had daughters and their daughters had daughters. The colony grew. Then came the Destruction. Our Grandmothers learned to live as if there were no machines and no Earth, conserving the machines they had left. Then the natives came from wherever they migrated from and their men killed some of us and raided our flocks. Our Grandmothers fought them off with weapons the First Mothers had brought. Our Grandmothers put up our fortifications and learned to fight like the native men did."

"You said they weren't hostile."

"They aren't, now. Not very. By the time the machines and the Earth weapons broke beyond repair, Our Mothers had earned their respect and learned to speak and trade with them. People who do those jobs," I said, patting my face to indicate I included myself, "are the lowest of the low. We have to deal with the males, you see."

"Males are bad," the Traveler said, as if he were paraphrasing a principle.

"My grandmother's grandmother told her that male births were an omen of lean times and disease."

"No!" He thumped his knees with his fists. If *I'd* done that, he would have complained about it. "No, male births were a *response* to lean times and disease! The natives decreased your freedom to expand your population, and competed with you for resources, so you started bearing males as well as females. That's how you were engineered. It cuts down on the rate of reproduction and mixes up the genetic material. It was supposed to happen. It had to happen."

I stood up and walked away. "We don't talk about these things."

The Traveler made a growly noise and shifted position. I crouched, prepared to meet his attack, but he stayed on the steps.

"We're not supposed to talk about it, either," he said. "To you, I mean. We're supposed to listen and learn. But I'm a biologist, not a sociologist, and we need to intervene or you'll die out in. . . well, not too many generations. So male births started to occur, and the Babas decided. . . . The Babas decided males were not wanted. Not allowed. Not allowed to . . .not allowed to. . . . When did the male births start? When did the Babas decide they couldn't happen?"

"In my mother's time. Some of that generation's babies were stillborn — more than the usual number, I mean. Some were males. My mother said the midwife didn't know what they were, but the Babas of that time knew. They decided. . . . Based on what they knew of the native men, they decided we didn't want any males. We didn't need them, and we didn't want them."

"So you do talk about these things among yourselves."

I shook my head. "We don't."

"But you just said—" He stopped speaking so abruptly, his tongue clicked against the roof of his mouth. "You asked, didn't you? You asked, and you just wouldn't stop asking until somebody answered. That's why they don't like you."

"That's one of the reasons."

"How many children have you had, personally, if you don't mind my asking?"

I knew he wasn't trying to shame me, so I swallowed hard and said, "None."

"And your mother, besides you?"

It took me a little longer to answer, "I have three sisters."

He heard what I didn't say.

"Did your mother have a stillborn male?"

I didn't answer. I was afraid of the next thing he'd guess.

"Did she have one born alive?"

When I was six, my mother had given birth earlier than expected. I was the only one home with her. The baby was her second male, only it was born alive. She and I looked at it in horror, then she turned away from it.

"I'll take care of it, Mama," I promised. "I'll take it out, myself, so you don't have to show it to anybody."

Males, I knew, were to be taken to the midden and left there dead — dead at birth or dead after birth, but dead. Dead and uncremated, dead and unhonored.

I met SharShar na Bal, who was then the youngest of the Babas, on the way.

"What do you have there?" she asked.

"Nothing important." I had wrapped it in a rag, and I clutched it close. I could feel its arms and legs squirming, its head turning back and forth as it rooted for milk. I almost dropped it, but I held on.

"Show it to me."

I couldn't. It was horrible, but it was mine. My mother didn't want it; I didn't want it, but it was mine. He was mine. A disgusting thing, but tiny and alive and sweet, somehow.

While I was gone, my older sisters and the midwife and SharShar na Bal visited my mother. Someone visited the midden and found neither my mother's male child nor me there. The day was overcast and windy, so no smoke would show from the Bowl, but I returned to furious reproaches for profaning a holy place. Because I was so young, I was only sentenced to six hours in The Turtle and was made to clean out the ash pit and throw the ashes on the midden. It was my first sentence, but it wasn't my last.

Now, the Traveler said, "You never thought the males should be killed, did you? You always knew males were people. You thought they should live with human respect and die. . . ." He choked on the words. "They should die with dignity."

"I'm tired," I said. "Please go away."

He did, which was good: I really was tired, and throwing people up the stairs is a lot harder than throwing them down them.

~*~

The next day, I wasn't surprised that the Babas didn't even remember sending the Traveler to me in The Turtle. He didn't mention it and neither did I.

I also wasn't surprised when one of the guards at the gate blew her horn and announced that a delegation of natives wanted to speak to the Babas. The coming of the visitors had shaken the balance between us, and the natives would be wanting to test and, if possible, exploit that.

The Babas were an inspiring sight, even to me, their loin wraps and their drapes rich with polished stone beads.

The native chief stood a little forward of the rest, as did SharShar na Bal.

She motioned me to stand behind her and translate.

The chief spat at the Baba's feet to show he was speaking to her and said (I translated), "You hold too much of the forest for your hunting grounds. We challenge you for the section between the river, the escarpment, the black rocks and the mountains." He had just claimed the best hunting grounds within two days' travel, and an enormous expanse of territory.

Bal laughed and clapped three times.

"You may not have the land," I translated.

"We challenge you for it!" he said, flushing a deep purple. "Your champion against ours, to the death, or we go to war!"

There had been no war in my memory — not in any of the Babas' memories. There had been many challenges on both sides, but our champions had always beaten theirs easily. They had brought males against us and, when they lost to our larger, stronger fighters, they had tried their females, who were trickier and more ruthless, but even smaller and weaker than their males.

"We will confer about this," I translated the Baba's words to the chief.

The Babas retreated into the meeting house. The Earth people were granted permission to attend, and our best fighters were called in as well. That included me.

"Their demand is out of the question," SharShar na Bal said flatly. "Someone must fight."

"But . . . to the death!" a younger Baba objected. "That's never been done. Not on purpose, at least! Why would they throw away their best fighter?"

"Who will go?" Bal asked.

Ordinarily, there would be a clamor for the honor of defeating the native champion. The death-challenge was daunting, though, and there were no volunteers.

"BranDal na Cam," Bal said, as I knew she would. "You will fight. They must have some secret or trick, or they wouldn't make this challenge. You other fighters, watch. See what the secret or the trick is. One of you will win when we challenge them to take the hunting grounds back."

The Earth people objected, but even I had to admit I was the most expendable of our fighters. It's possible I even deserved it. A troublemaker from the womb, it's as if I had been born for exactly this.

~*~

The fight would be held in a clearing beyond the Mountain Gate. Barbara, Chandra and the Traveler insisted on coming so Barbara could transmit the "event". They looked solemn and grim, as if death were a strange and frightening thing. I wasn't looking forward to it, myself. I was a callous opponent in a fight, but fighting is one thing and killing is another.

I wore a leather breast binder and leather wrist guards. I was barefoot and carried a shield of stiffened hide on my left arm and a bronze sword in my right hand.

The natives' head man and his retinue were already standing on their side of the clearing when the Babas and their honor guard and the visitors and I arrived.

The head man came forward.

"Present your champion," he said.

I walked to the center of the clearing.

SharShar na Bal said, "Present your challenger."

The head man stepped back and held up a three-fingered hand, upper lip lifted in a disquieting grimace of satisfaction.

A giant strode out of the forest. He stood at least two heads higher than any of the other natives — and taller than any of us — almost as tall as the Traveler. He was bare from the waist up, and painted all over with auburn nut-pod juice and white clay. Even his head was shaved and painted. He carried a stone knife and a heavy wooden club; lizardskin mittens gripped his crude weapons.

We came face-to-face in the circle our peoples made around us. I glared defiantly up into his big face and saw, with a shock, that his eyes were brown, like a person's, not red or yellow, like the other natives'. I saw shock on his face, too—I was probably the first fighter in a long time who dared to face him voluntarily.

He would be strong, and he was bigger than I was, but I wasn't overly worried about it: We have fight training from childhood up, with the best fighters continuing and training the younger girls. That meant I had trained for fighting people smaller than I am, but it also meant that my earliest training was against larger and stronger opponents.

"Withdraw!" I shouted, according to established ritual.

"Yield!" he replied, his voice not as deep as the Traveler's, but deeper than any other I had ever heard.

We each backed away and spat, then kicked dust over one another's spittle, signaling that the battle was engaged.

The giant raised his club, but hesitated, no doubt unused to an opponent anywhere close to his own size.

I took advantage, shoving my shield up toward his eyes and slicing at his kneecap with my sword. I came in under my target, but opened a shallow wound across his shin. Blood poured down over his foot.

Red blood, not purple.

I danced back out of his reach while I recovered from the surprise. I wanted to look around, to see if anyone else saw what I saw, but I didn't dare take my eyes off him. I didn't hear any sounds of amazement, so I told myself I must be wrong. The blood was purple. It had to be purple.

He lunged with his knife. I parried, sliding my blade down his and shaving the top of his lizardskin mitten right off his hand. He swung his cudgel and clipped me on the shoulder as I dodged. I felt the blow deep in my muscle, but it missed the bone.

The giant was fast, and he had a lot of power behind his blows.

Block their line of sight and cut their legs out from under them; that had done the job for me when I was young, and I worked it for all it was worth now.

I clipped him on the nose with the edge of my shield and heard him grunt with pain. He came in for a sideswipe to my neck with his razor-honed stone knife and I tasted the cut rather than felt it, a metallic tang in the roof of my mouth as I smelled my own blood.

I feinted with the shield. He leaned away from it and I leapt into the air and brought my weight in behind a kick to his knee. I felt his kneecap pop out of place, and he went down, howling, his cudgel flying one way and his knife another.

For the second time in as many days, I straddled a man, his life in my hands, this time with the point of my sword at his throat.

His face was smeared with sweat and blood — red blood. Yes! Red! And that look of shock was back — had never really left.

"Yield," I whispered. He put his hands together in token of submission.

"Kill him!" my people shouted, and his people shouted, "Kill him!"

I dropped my sword and tore his lizardskin mittens off. His hands had thumbs and three fingers, as natives should have . . . and scars, where his fourth fingers had been cut off, probably when he was an infant.

I rose, still standing astride the giant's body.

"I claim this man's life," I said. "I defeated him, did I not?"

My people affirmed it loudly, and none of the natives disputed it. "I claim him, and I will *not* kill him. This man," I said, turning to the Babas and shouting my assertion, "is my sister."

~*~

"Brother," the Traveler said, back in the meeting house. "This man is your *brother*."

"What have you done?" BrenCar na Den asked.

"It seems to me like she's saved your bacon," the Traveler said.

The Babas didn't answer — didn't seem to hear.

"I did a good thing," I said, looking to the Traveler, to make sure I had understood his meaning. He nodded and gave me a wicked grin. It threw me a little off-balance, having an ally against the Babas. "I was right," I said. "Males are people, too. We were supposed to bear them and use them to reproduce. They were supposed to make us stronger and healthier. More and more of us are barren because we rejected this gift the First Mothers meant us to have. And *I* didn't kill one." I struck my chest. "*I* didn't. *Me*."

For the first time in my life, SharShar na Bal was speechless. Not for long, though.

"You didn't take him to the Bowl," she said. "You took the punishment for defiling the Resting Place, but. . . ."

"But I didn't kill him and burn his body with the Mothers. I hid him in a hollow tree in the forest. After I was let out of The Turtle, I went back with food and water, but he was gone. I thought a wild animal had taken him to raise. When I grew older, I thought a wild animal had taken him to *eat*. Now I suppose a native saw me and carried him home as a prize."

"And they raised him in secret and used him against us!" said Den.

"I did a *good* thing!" I insisted.

"Yes," said Bal. "You did."

". . .I did?"

She looked away. "The old Babas were wrong. I always thought so." She glanced at me with a wry smile. "I had too much respect for their wisdom and age to question them, but I questioned them in my heart."

I thought it was just like her to side with me as soon as I was vindicated, and to claim she had been on my side since before I was born.

She went on: "They let fear garble the wisdom of the First Mothers, and passed down to us a truth so twisted it became a lie. The First Mothers would be happy to know the Earth didn't forget us, and they would be happy that their truth has been made clear again."

The Babas' honor guard flicked murderous glances from the Traveler to me. I could imagine what they were thinking, because I was thinking it too.

"Traveler," I said, "if we promise to let all males born to us live, could you help us have strong babies without conjugation?"

"Uh. . . . Not me, personally. . . . In the future, you mean. Yes. Yes. It's a simple technology, to use sperm from males to artificially inseminate females."

Chandra smirked. "But you may find that girls who grow

up around boys might not be entirely opposed to . . . conjugating with them."

"That," said SharShar na Bal, "will be some other Babas' problem."

"On the other hand," Den said to me, "you, not to mention that *thing* you brought back from the fight, are *our* problem."

I saw her point. My sister — my *brother* — had been raised by barbarians. I had no idea what kind of life he had led among them, but I was certain he wouldn't fit into our culture. I knew *I* never had.

The Traveler whispered to Chandra, who said, "I can ask." Then she excused herself, stepped away from us and spoke into her device. We looked glumly at one another, waiting for her to finish and rejoin the discussion.

Perhaps the rest of my people were thinking, as I was, of life with an uncivilized male in our midst. Would he have to be confined? Would he live in The Turtle, or would he be put in a quarantine hut, as if he had a disease our healers didn't know how to cure? Would he be taught how to behave? *Could* he be taught? Would he feel the urge to reproduce, as people do? When he felt that urge, that longing, how would he respond?

Chandra came back to us, nodding and smiling.

"Earth wants me to ask you a tremendous favor," she told the Babas. "We were going to wait to ask, until we had been here longer and had given you time to know us and trust us, but I've been given permission to ask now."

"Ask," Bal said, when I had translated what she understood as well as I did. Babas!

"Many parthenogenetic pioneers were sent out," Chandra said, "but all of them have fluctuated between sexual and asexual reproduction, depending on their circumstances. You've maintained parthenogenesis. Earth is very interested in studying your psychology and physiology, especially your reproductive attitudes and systems."

The Traveler blushed, for some reason.

Chandra didn't notice, and went on. "It's wonderfully fortunate that there's now a male we can study as well."

Bal said, without waiting for me to translate, "A brother and sister would make an excellent comparison, don't you think?"

"I do," said Chandra.

I gaped until my jaw cracked and I had to shut my mouth. My heart thudded with terror and delight. *Leave? Leave my home? Leave my people? Leave The Turtle that we had built for ourselves out of a misunderstood past and a guilty present? Oh, yes!*

"We have the facilities for the study on the ship, in orbit around this planet." Chandra turned to me and said, "It won't hurt. I promise you it won't. It will only be for a few days, two weeks at the most, and then we'll bring you right back."

Just long enough for the Babas to decide how to cope with the male I hadn't killed. Disappointment flooded me, and I blurted out, "I don't get to go to Earth?"

Chandra looked happy as she said, "Would you like to? Would you do that?"

"I would. I would like that. I would do that."

"What about your brother?"

I snorted. "He'll do as I tell him."

~*~

The Traveler and Chandra and I went to the shuttle, where NolaSara na Barbara was tending to my *brother*.

As we entered, he smiled proudly at me. "You fight well,"

he said, in the native tongue.

"I fight like a girl," I agreed.

"I let you win," he said.

"Like stink," I said. "When you recover, I'll beat you again."

He shook his head, but he smiled.

Barbara had washed him and now it was easy to see our mother's features, even though his nose was starting to swell from my tagging him with my shield. No wonder he had been startled, to look at me and see his own face looking back.

Barbara finished wrapping a bandage around his wounded leg and said, "He calls himself Tomma."

"Native for 'monster'," I said.

"Sounds like Tomas," the Traveler said. "My father's name was Tomas. My name is Pablo, you know. Pablo Huertos."

"My *brother's* name," I said, "is also Tomas. That's an Earth name. He comes from the First Mother Bran. His mother is Dal. His name is BranDal na Tomas."

"Then," said the Traveler, "my name is. . . ," he thought, as the Earth people — the *other* Earth people — had, reaching for the earliest female relative's name he could remember, "JacintaConsuela na Pablo. Can you say that? Try."

I ignored him, then looked at him and nodded. "JacintaConsuela na Pablo." Ignoring people was what the Babas did. I never wanted to become a Baba.

Other Earth, Other Stars

Prior publication information

Solo For Multiple Instruments – FUTURE PERFECT, TENSE IN SPACE, 2010

Out of the Frying Pan – #amwriting website, 2012

Prime Date – Quills and Quibbles website, 2011

Treasure of the Terra Madre – Marian Allen, Author Lady website, 2014

Best Ride in Space – Marian Allen, Author Lady website, 2014

Craw – Quills and Quibbles website, 2011

Line of Descent – Smashwords, Kindle, since withdrawn

Out of the Cradle – BEASTLY TALES, 2006

Blood of Mermayds – Marian Allen, Author Lady website, since withdrawn

Becalmed at Sea – Marian Allen, Author Lady website, 2014

SMILE, Mr. President – Marian Allen, Author Lady website, 2014

Three Men in a Blimp, To Say Nothing of the Automaton – CIRCUITS AND STEAM, 2014

Dog Star – WorldWide Recipes newsletter, 2003; NOVEL INGREDIENTS, 2003

Sure Thing – Quills and Quibbles website, 2013

Pile-Up – Race to the Hugo Award website, 2013

Snow on the Screen – Marian Allen, Author Lady website, 2015

A Long Time Coming – Marian Allen, Author Lady website, 2015

Western Star – Marian Allen, Author Lady website, 2015

Aardvark With an Arrow – #amwriting website, 2012

Reading From the Book of First Bambi – Marian Allen, Author Lady website, 2014

Slob vs Snob – Marian Allen, Author Lady website, 2013

The One and Only – Marian Allen, Author Lady website, 2013

Til Death Us Do Part – Race to the Hugo Award website, 2014

The Woman Who Wasn't a Shave-Tail – Oceans of the Mind website, 2002

Demon Ozone – Yandro, 1979; PAIR OF NORMAL WHAT, 2013

Sanctuary – Quills and Quibbles website, 2011

About the Author

For as long as she can remember, Marian Allen has loved telling and being told stories. When, at the age of about six, she was informed that somebody got paid for writing all those books and movies and television shows, she abandoned her previous ambition (beachcomber), and became a writer.